FORBIDDEN DREAMS

Forbidden Love Book 2

ROSE FRESQUEZ

ISBN: 978-1-961159-24-2

Copyright © 2025 by Rose Fresquez

All rights reserved. Except for use in any review, the reproduction or utilization of this work in whole or in part in any form by any electronic, mechanical or other means, now known or hereafter invented, including photocopying and recording, or in any information storage retrieval system, is forbidden without the written permission of the publisher.

Forbidden Dreams is a work of fiction. Names, characters, places, and incidents are either the product of the author's imagination or are used fictitiously, and any resemblance to actual persons, living or dead, business establishments, events or locales is entirely coincidental.

Join my Insider Group and get an exclusive Novella, THE THERAPIST'S NEIGH-BOR

DEDICATION

*To my mother, **Harriet Namirimu**, and my father, **James Mudoba**, now in heaven.*

Mama Harriet, thank you for your kindness and for listening when God called. Your faith opened the door to my own journey with Christ, and I carry that legacy with me every day.

Papa James, thank you for choosing a different path. While many in the village raised their sons to farm and their daughters to prepare for marriage, you sacrificed everything—working tirelessly so that my siblings and I could go to school.

This story is my way of revisiting the beautiful memories and the legacy you left behind. I thank God that in His perfect plan, He chose you to be my parents.

ACKNOWLEDGEMENTS

I want to thank the Lord, my Savior. Without you, Father, there's no point in trying to do anything at all. It's my prayer that I can honor you with my words. I thank you for connecting me with an amazing group of people who helped support me in accomplishing this novel.

To my husband Joel, who works so hard to provide for our family, so that I can stay home and take care of the kids. I'm so blessed that we get to journey through life together.

To my children Isaiah, Caleb, Abigail and Micah, you fill my heart with joy. Thanks for the giggles, laughter and encouragement.

To my editor, Deirdre Lockhart. You're a true blessing from God. Your insights and wisdom have helped shape this story.

And to GOD, Who makes everything possible. Without God's wisdom and creativity, this story wouldn't be in existence.

To my Beta team, Carol , Sylvia, Trudy, Debby, John and Anna. Thanks for reading the raw manuscript and suggesting incredible ideas.

To my Street Team. Thank you from the bottom of my heart.

CHAPTER 1

THE OUTSIDER

Fred

Outsider. It could be a wound to some. But I've learned to wear it like armor—years at home prepared me for it.

I swing the slasher through the tall grass, sweat slicking my brow. The sun drapes long shadows over the field, gilding every blade in gold and green. Each swing crushes weeds, releasing their scent into the thick air. This patch by the fence needs to be cleared today. Exams begin tomorrow and will last for two weeks.

"Fred."

I stand and turn, wiping sweat from my forehead with the back of my hand.

Headmaster John Lugire strides my way. Tie loosened, sleeves rolled, as always. He has to remain dressed fancy until the pupils are in bed. His brown eyes are kind, but his brows are furrowed.

"I thought we agreed." He stops a few metres away. "Work ends when the supper bell rings. After that, you study."

"I know, sir." I square my shoulders, toss the slasher with a thud into the grass. "I didn't want to leave this area unfinished."

For six months, I've been at St. Anthony Secondary School. The air here smells of grass, not the soil I used to dig through in our fields. Chalk dust lingers in the corridors. At night, when most pupils sleep, I sit in the empty classroom to catch up on my studying. Hired here to cut the grass and pull weeds, I'm also allowed to study. Thus, I don't attend classes like the others.

But some afternoons, John tutors me in the subjects I struggle with most—Math, where numbers blur like heat waves, and English, where verbs mock me. For History, Geography, and the rest, I rely on the textbooks Lucy sent me.

That box arrived one day, shipped to the headmaster. Heavy and taped in layers. Inside, lay stacks of study guides, but past the papers, she included a packet of sweets with a note: "Only eat one after finishing a full subject."

Turns out the books are the same curriculum St. Anthony uses. John always points out the units I should be studying.

Now, he sighs, scratching at his head. His short black hair hides the gray in the fading light. "You're not here to win a landscaping award, Fred. You know how important UCE is."

A smile tugs at my mouth. "I'll catch up tonight. Promise."

The Uganda Certificate of Education, the national exam, is taken at the end of senior four. Most students take it at sixteen. I'm doing it at eighteen. Thanks to Lucy, the headmaster, and his wife, Gertrude, for holding me this far.

"You're still aware exams start tomorrow, right?"

"Yes, sir."

"Since you already made me supper, come on. Let's share it before you go study. The grass can wait till tomorrow night."

"Yes, sir." I'd rather finish the job tonight. But arguing with him won't get me anywhere. So I gather the slasher and sling it over my shoulder. The field hums behind me—crickets starting their chorus.

The electric bell rings, different from the clanging metal supper bell.

Delighted squeals burst from the dining building. Through its open windows rises a wild song of clanging metal plates and chattering students. Boys and girls, most younger than me, march toward the dorms.

One boy stands under a nakalira tree. The orange and red blooms from overhanging branches dust his shoulders. He leans close to a girl, saying something low as she laughs and looks down. Their arms don't touch, but the space between them sizzles with everything they're not allowed to say.

An ache intrudes. Lucy could be standing under a tree like that now, talking to a boy who belongs in her world—someone clever with smooth words. Not some farm boy like me.

The headmaster eyes me a beat longer. Then his mouth twitches like he wants to smile but won't let himself.

My stomach growls. It's suppertime for me too, I guess.

The staff quarters have stucco siding and red roofs as opposed to the brick classes and pupils' housing.

Before following John into the house, I set the slasher on the veranda and wash my hands. The bulb flickers. Tonight better not end in another blackout. I could use more time memorizing schoolwork.

Whew. When I enter the two-bedroom house, the bulb above the dining table isn't flickering. The scent of groundnuts and mushrooms dominates the sweet potatoes we will be eating. The headmaster brings the food to the table and ushers me to the empty folding wooden chair across from him.

"How did you learn to cook like this?" John breaks a potato and dips it in the peanut sauce.

I laugh, shifting in the chair as I reach for a potato. "I've seen my mother cook. I figured, how hard could it be?"

"It's not men's work to take interest in the kitchen."

"Looks like you'll be starving since your wife isn't here to cook." I dip my potato into the sauce.

"Gertrude knows you're cooking for me. Otherwise, she'd be coming by three times a week to cook for me."

I chuckle, grateful to know not all marriages lack real love and connection like my father and mother.

I ask about John's day as I do whenever we have supper together. Sometimes I cook and leave for my quarters, but other days, he insists I join him.

"There's always something." John reaches for another potato and breaks it. "That teacher again. Still refusing to use the new attendance system. I was hesitant to use technology too, but it does wonders once you get used to it."

"I wouldn't know much about machines." I pause to chew my potato. "The most I've done is try to fix a broken radio."

He chuckles. "Even that's more than some teachers here are willing to try."

I laugh in the right places, licking the sauce from my fingers. It's easy to side with him—even if technology is still foreign to me. Though I know one thing it's good for. "It comes in handy when Lucy calls. That's reason enough to support it."

"Lucy called earlier, by the way."

My heart whooshes, and I freeze midbite. "She did?"

"She wanted to wish you luck."

I swallow down the longing to be in her presence. "Will she call again?"

"That was the only time she could sneak the phone today."

A plus side of being close to the headmaster? He has a phone, and he's not Lucy's headmaster. Otherwise, he'd have confiscated her phone by now. Sometimes when she calls, I'm lucky, John finds me, and I get to hear her voice.

I can't ever call back. If her phone rings at the wrong time, her teachers will confiscate it until the end of the term.

It's later that night, after I've cleaned and settled into my one-room cabin beyond the staff quarters. The concrete floor is cool under my bare feet, and the single bulb dangling from a wire casts just enough light.

I could touch my bed with the reach of my hand. The place reminds me of my cozy hut back home—except this one has electricity and walls that don't breathe dust.

I flip through my photo album, each picture a memory—me and Lucy beneath mango trees, Viola balancing a pot on her head, Lucy's younger siblings chasing chickens barefoot. All taken during the only holiday Lucy ever spent in the village. Before her father forbade her from returning.

With her face fresh in my mind, I press play on the small radio CD player next to my bed. The disc whirs to life.

"Imagine you're there." Lucy's melody floats through the room like a breeze through leaves—soft, confident, teasing. "Mercury's the closest one, fast and dry and full of sun. Venus spins the other way, bright and hot. Don't ever stay."

She sent me this song before third term started to keep me focused when missing her got too loud. Music's the best way my brain holds onto facts, and my extraordinary Lucy knows that.

The room darkens. A blackout. Typical. The radio still plays, crackling through the silence. Power should return by midnight, hopefully.

The wooden chair squeaks when I shift. Good thing I stocked up on batteries.

Now, the humming radio blends with the distant chirping crickets and the occasional hooting owl.

"Jupiter's storms and Saturn's rings, Neptune's cold and Uranus leans..."

I close my eyes, and Lucy's voice carries me. I'm no longer in this box of a room. I'm lying on the hill on her expansive property, grass prickling my arms, her shoulder brushing mine, the sky wide and full of stars.

After Astronomy, I pat the table in the dark, fingers landing on the torch. Its beam slices through the shadows as I swap the disc, switching to the English CD. Her voice floats out, turning grammar into lullabies.

I click replay. At some point, the power surges back, and light floods the room. I flip through my notes and maps, reciting the capital cities I always forget.

By midnight, my eyes sting, but I have a good feeling I'm ready for Astronomy, Geography, and English tomorrow.

When I drift off, I dream of quizzes and test papers, every line of text forming into Lucy's handwriting. Then I wake to a clatter at my door and leap out of bed to open the door.

"Headmaster." I yawn.

"I wanted to make sure you don't skip breakfast." He hands me a flask and a grease-stained newspaper wrapping with what seems like mandazi. The savory scent is unmistakable. "I hope you have a cup to drink your tea."

"Thank you." My voice comes out raspy with sleep. I hadn't planned to eat, but I'm grateful. "I still have my cup." I rarely drink tea. Takes a lot of time to fix.

After he leaves, I eat, then don the school uniform for the first time—a crisp white shirt with the crest stitched on the pocket and navy blue trousers still stiff from tailoring. It smells new. Feels like possibility.

With no mirror in my room, I've got no clue how I look. Which makes me wonder just how strange I must seem, especially when I step into the classroom and every head turns. Thirty-some pupils, boys and girls, gawk.

"Find the desk with your name," instructs the exam supervisor. From the national board, he's not one of St. Anthony's teachers. Neutral, to keep things fair.

Schools with high scores gain prestige, funding, and increased enrollment. Without outside supervision, teachers could easily bend the rules.

The air inside is dense, and the clock's regular tick drags across my skin like a cold breeze.

Sheets are passed out. Pencils and pens are laid neatly.

"When the bell rings," the supervisor says, "you may begin."

Another instructor walks in, scanning the room for movement.

The bell tolls. Pencils lift. Papers flip. The scent of fresh ink and paper hits me like a punch of clarity.

The first exam is English.

I don't expect to walk away with confidence. But I do what Lucy advised. Start with what I know.

One essay catches my eye: Write about a day you'll never forget.

A smile creeps up. Easy. I write about Jinja. The Nile. The sound of rushing water and the feel of Lucy's hand in mine. I don't use her name—just say "my best friend." I can't risk sounding like a boy too in love to focus.

There's an argumentative essay about telephones. I've never owned one, but I know what it feels like to need one. For Lucy. The words come easier than my hand can keep up with.

Then a formal letter. I pretend I'm writing to someone else, but I picture Lucy reading every line.

The afternoon is Astronomy.

When I see the question on constellations, my heart nearly bursts. I'm back on that hill with the telescope she left me. The Great and Little Bears, the Herdsman, Leo the Lion, Draco the Dragon, Cepheus the King, Cassiopeia the Queen, even Camelopardalis the Giraffe. Her voice plays in my head like a cheat code. I answer with a grin.

Stars. Seasons. Planetary movement.

I fly through it.

That rhythm carries me through the next two weeks.

Agriculture is a breeze. It's my life back in the village. Bonus points when a question on irrigation pops up. During that holiday with Lucy, both of us read about the right method to use in our fields. I don't garden at all during exam weeks. Just study. Memorize. Repeat.

Physics nearly kills me. Math tries to, but I survive.

By the time I sit for the final paper, I'm not even tired. I'm wired—focused, already thinking ahead to the senior-six exams.

But first, I need to see Lucy.

How? I don't know yet. But I have to.

CHAPTER 2

THE TRANSITION VISIT

Lucy

"Out, out, out!" I order. "Assembly's not optional unless you're dead or dying!"

I weave through the jungle of double and triple beds, navigating a floor littered with socks, worn textbooks, and nuts. Mosquito nets hang half tied like ghostly curtains, and morning light seeps through slatted windows. Metal suitcases slam shut, their clang ringing in the dorm room.

"You two already know the drill. Move!" I wag my finger between two girls seated on opposite bottom bunks, deep in chatter like the schedule just fell from the sky. "If you're late, you'll be on bathroom duty again."

"Can we skip today, please?" asks the girl with a bald haircut, her eyes hopeful. Her friend waits for my reaction like this is some game of bluff.

"Not today." I steel my voice, though they know better. If they didn't, they wouldn't keep trying. They shuffle out, giggling.

My trainee, Doreen, edges closer. Just a couple inches shorter, she somehow carries herself taller. Her gaze is sharp, spine straight, eyes scanning like she owns the corridor already. Born for this, clearly. Unlike me. I've led all year and still second-guess every step.

She stops beside a top bunk, frowns, then lifts a lumpy blanket. And uncovers the girl curled beneath it, feigning invisibility. "Why are you still sleeping?"

"I don't feel so well today."

"Then why aren't you in the dispensary?" Doreen's brow lifts.

The girl flinches.

I sigh. Poor thing. I touch her knee, softening my voice. "You can't miss another day of school."

"Just Mr. Luya's class."

Of course. "You'll be in a new class next year. Hang in there."

She groans and drags her suitcase from the foot of her bed.

We finish our patrol. The scent of damp shoes, powerful body spray, and last night's boiled beans hits me. A girl snaps a towel off her bed, slams her trunk shut, and thuds her suitcase onto the floor.

"These S1s and 2s think the dorm is a hotel." I dodge a sock. "But we need to be patient and let them learn."

"That's not what my dorm prefect taught me." Doreen's face hardens. "These children need a firmer tone than you're giving them."

"I'm not here to make enemies." I step over a half-zipped back-pack in the long corridor.

Girls scurry out, white blouses tucked into army-green skirts, socks sliding down their calves. Haircuts range from clean buzz cuts to out-of-shape tight curls begging for a trim.

Once we confirm the dorms for the young pupils are clear, we move to the S3 and S4 blocks and repeat the same.

By the time we reach the assembly field outside the administrative offices, the sun is warming the horizon. The grass is patchy, red earth showing through where hundreds of feet have trampled during games of kwepena. Birds chirp from a nearby deciduous tree, their songs rising above the pupils' low murmurs.

As prefects, we don't stand in line. We scan the crowd, making sure everyone's in proper uniform. On the cemented assembly square, boys and girls line up by class, their white blouses reflecting the morning sun.

David, the boys' dorm prefect, watches from across the way, smirking like always. Once upon a time, I had a crush on him and would've melted at that look. Now, with my heart tethered to Fred, it barely stirs a flicker when I smile back.

A clap of hands brings my attention back. The headmistress steps back, and another teacher moves forward to lead prayers.

"Bless the efforts of our hard work..."

My mind drifts to someone working harder than any of us. I tried calling Fred yesterday to ask how UCE went, but John didn't pick up. Fred sacrificed his relationship with his father to study. I hope his efforts pay off.

Voices rise for the closing song. I join in. I've already said my morning prayers like I do every day as soon as I wake up and before I go to bed. I need God to help Fred pass the national exams. And myself as well, switching from art subjects for my clothing design to sciences wasn't easy. But I need to be a doctor.

Like Mama says, only God knows how things will turn out.

I love starting the day with biology—my brain is still fresh enough to keep up. We're halfway through a lesson on plant cells when a knock on the open door cuts the teacher off midsentence. Every head turns.

The assistant headmaster stands framed in the doorway. The headmistress and her assistant only walk into the classroom to fetch someone for a matter in the main office. Which explains why everyone, including the teacher, remains silent.

"Lucy Sanyu?"

I straightened, my pen paused midword on the sentence about chloroplasts.

"Yes, sir?"

"You have a visitor at the office."

My heart lurches. I got pulled out like this when Papa came to tell me my baby sister died.

"Maybe it's your father," my desk mate Cici whispers. "He missed visiting day."

But that wasn't the first visiting day Papa missed.

I slide back my chair, and it creaks against the cement. I plant one foot in front of the other and inch for the door.

"Are you ready for the exams next week?" the assistant headmaster asks as we head down the veranda.

"Yes," I lie. I've stayed up late studying, memorizing diagrams, formulas, and diseases. But I still don't feel ready.

The administration block rises at the edge of the compound, sunlight glinting off its glass windows. November brings more sun than the rain-soaked September and early October, and I'm grateful for it.

Marigolds and hibiscus line the paved path, their colors bright against the trimmed grass. Bougainvillea climbs the brick wall, and the air smells sweet—fresh, floral, and warm. It all reminds me of Fred.

He keeps the grounds at his school just as neat. Since last term, flowers like these make me think of him.

"I need a snack," the assistant headmaster says, then veers off toward the staff room, sending me to the headmistress's office.

My feet pound the brick path up the steps to the office. The door is half open. When I knock, a feminine voice calls me to come in.

I step into the reception, and my eyes widen. My stomach flutters, and my heart beats faster. "Fred?"

He grins—that crooked, confident smile I've missed more than I'd like to admit. He stands from the wooden bench beneath the whirring fan. The overhead light flickers above his head. His shoulders stretch out a crisp white shirt, its sleeves rolled. "His belt's seen better days, and his shoes shine so hard it's like he polished them with cooking oil.

"You? How did you...?" I lift my hands and move closer to hug him, but the scratch of the chair against the cement has me pausing. Oh, right. We have an audience. I catch the secretary rising from behind her desk. I hadn't noticed she was there.

"Good morning, Mrs. Kisu," I greet her breathlessly.

She gives a curt nod. "Keep your visit short, please. It's not a visiting day."

"Fred is family." I reply too fast, like I'm trying to convince myself more than her. Panic flutters again. How did he get past the gatekeeper?

A voice floats from the open office door behind us. The headmistress. She's clearly on the phone, but her presence casts a shadow over the whole room.

"How did you even get in here?" I whisper.

"I told them we're kind of family," he replies just as quietly, a mischievous glint lighting his face. "Had to tell them your parents' names and siblings."

We sit at the edge of the bench, careful—like intruders in a sacred space. I slide my hand to his waist, my gaze flicking to the secretary scribbling on a stack of envelopes. Fred's arm wraps behind me, and warmth spreads through my chest. He's solid, familiar. He smells like soap and home, and all the dusty memories of Busobi village rush back.

"I missed you," I whisper into his shoulder.

"Me the most." His warm breath brushes my ear and sets my skin ablaze.

We pull back.

I search his face. "How did your exams go?"

"I think I did very well."

My chest lifts. "You feel good about it?"

He beams. "Astronomy had the whole solar system. It was like you wrote the exam yourself."

I laugh. "I'm glad my songs came through."

His eyes soften as he peers into mine. I peek to ensure the secretary isn't on to us. Last thing I need is my father finding out Fred visited me. The secretary is still busy. Whew.

"Your voice... it helped me focus."

My cheeks burn. I check the headmistress's door next. She's no longer speaking, but papers rustle.

"We've only got a week until UACE," I whisper. "Do you feel prepared?"

Fred nods. "The study guides you gave me make this manageable. I'm only worried about Economics. But Divinity and Geography? I can handle those."

"At least we both get to do Economics together." I slide my hand into his, keeping them between my skirt folds where my skirt rubs against his pants. Our time is hanging by a thread. "Think of my brother's business skills. Alex is always doing business with you. Plus, you're practically a businessman already with the crops you take to town."

He chuckles, that deep belly sound I missed so much. He lifts our entwined hands and peeks at the secretary under his brows, then the headmistress's door. He then brings our hands to his mouth and kisses my fingertips, gaze focused on the secretary.

I cackle, despite the sizzle humming through me at his lips touching my flesh. "Since when did you get this bold?"

His mischievous grin crinkles up his eyes. "Since Lucy came into my life." He says it like I'm the most important person in his life. "I miss you so much."

"I'm planning to come see you right after the exams." That was my plan all along. Finish exams, visit Fred at St. Anthony's, then go back to Papa's workplace for my holidays.

"I'd love to see you." Longing leaves his voice husky. Then concern slips into his expression. "Has your papa changed his mind about you coming to the village?"

"Papa still doesn't want me back in the village." That sits like a stone in my chest. "He found a hospital near Kampala where I'll be shadowing during the holidays."

The secretary steps out of the office, and I breathe in relief. Although the headmistress isn't too far, she's not staring at us, at least.

"What's shadowing?"

"Observing. Following a nurse or doctor through their work. Learning by watching, not doing yet. Like being an apprentice but without touching patients."

Fred's smile doesn't meet his face. "So we won't see each other during the holiday?"

"We'll find a way." Not sure how, but we will.

He stares ahead, jaw working. The laugh he lets out doesn't quite fit his face, either. "Then I'd better pass. So I can get a sponsorship and go to the institute close to where you'll be."

"You'll pass." He's too determined not to. Sponsorships are the only way forward for him.

Footsteps approach. We tear our hands apart, both jerking as the headmistress exits her office, files tucked under her arm. She doesn't seem to notice us, thankfully, as she walks to the door, heels clicking on cement.

The second she's gone, I grab Fred's arm and pull him toward her office.

"What are you—"

I silence him when I lean in and press my lips to his. He stumbles forward, and his hand cups my face as he kisses me. He smells of mint, and I savor the warmth, toes curling, so does my hand around his neck. The kiss isn't as long as I want it, but enough to silence every aching moment from the last months.

Fred, always the sensible one, pulls us apart. He blinks, stunned. "You—you kissed me in the headmistress's office?"

Then he kisses me again, this time sure and warm. When he pulls back, he takes my arm with him and rushes me back to the bench.

The secretary reappears. Her eyes scan us, suspicion behind her glasses.

Fred clears his throat and stands. "I best get going."

"Yes." Breathless, pulse still racing, I wobble to my feet.

He bows and thanks the secretary for her help. Then we walk together to the gate, our fingers brushing once, then again, but never quite locking.

"I'll be praying for you," I whisper. "UACE's no joke."

"Me too. I know my passing isn't just about becoming a teacher." He gives me a sidelong glance, voice dipping. "I'm still not sure why you want someone like me."

I smile, masking the ache rising in my throat. "I could say the same."

"Regardless of what happens..." He gulps, his voice strained. "I'll wait for you, Lucy. Yes, your course will take longer now. But you're worth the wait."

Our steps slow at the big metal gate, padlocked tight. The uniformed watchman steps out of his booth and unlocks the smaller gate, glancing between us.

We stand there, neither of us daring to show what we feel. A glance. A breath. I want to throw my arms around him and say goodbye. But I can't without getting us both in trouble.

Fred reaches into his pocket and checks to make sure the guard isn't looking before he pulls out something red.

"It's all crumpled." He winces and steps in to shield his treasure from the gatekeeper.

"A dahlia." My lower lip curls up, and my heart warms.

"I'd have brought a bouquet, but I wanted to keep my presence as a family member rather than a boyfriend."

"I love it." I steal it from his hand, and my heart squeezes as I sniff it. Then I thrust it into my skirt pocket so I don't get questioned. "I can still enjoy the petals."

"If you come to the village again, I'll take you back to the field."

Tears sting, and I speak through the lump rising in my throat. "I'm counting on that."

Fred starts toward the gate without looking back. Only when he reaches the other side does he pause and turn, lips pressed into a sad smile.

I lift my hand to wave. He mirrors it—slow, reluctant, like it costs him something.

My entire body weak, I force one foot in front of the other back to class. Did his visit help or ruin me? Now, all I want is to break every rule, sneak out for two nights, and see him again. Just talk.

Long distance hurts.

CHAPTER 3

THE END BEFORE THE BEGINNING

Fred

Seeing Lucy was like rain after drought—exactly what I needed to thrive before facing the Uganda Advanced Certificate of Education (UACE). Her face stays with me through each paper, hope against doubt. I'm not certain how I'm performing, but I'll make it. I have to. My future, my siblings' education, my possibility of a life with Lucy—all of it depends on these exams.

With her promising we'll meet after our finals, I renew my determination and push through the last papers. When I finish my final exam almost two weeks later, I celebrate in anticipation of seeing her soon. Whether I've done well enough for a sponsorship is another question, but I've given everything I have.

Before noon, I change out of my uniform and head straight to the grounds. The air hangs thick with humidity—the kind that clings to your skin before rain. If it pours, this might be the last rain before December's dry stretch.

The sun isn't harsh, but the heavy air keeps sweat clinging to me as I tackle the overgrown grass along the compound's edge. The flowers don't need attention—they bloom in neat beds, splashes of red and purple bright against weathered cement walls.

I've kept the bougainvillea trimmed. They get wild if I don't stay ahead of them. I swing the slasher, clearing the last strip. But there's always that one hard-to-reach spot under the metal fence. I'll need the trimmer for it.

"Fred! Fred!" Headmaster John rushes toward me, waving a phone.

My heart leaps. Lucy is the only one who calls me.

"Here you go." He passes it over, slightly out of breath.

My hands tremble. He gives a knowing nod and steps away, granting me privacy. The breeze cooling me, I walk to the umbrella-shaped tree—I didn't know umbrellas until I saw them here at school.

"Lucy." I breathe her name like a prayer.

"Oh, Fred." Her voice catches. Something must be wrong. "I'm so sorry. I can't come to see you."

The words slam into my chest like a brick. I grip the phone tighter as a purple flower drifts from the branches.

"Papa knew when my exams would finish." Her words tumble out in a rush. "He was so excited about my observation sessions that he wanted me to start right away. He came to get me yesterday the moment I stepped out after my last paper. I didn't even have time to call you."

I swallow hard. "Where are you now?"

"At the hospital, can you believe it? Papa drove me straight here to meet everyone as soon as we arrived." Frustration hangs in her voice. "I started the shadowing program today already. Everything's happening so fast."

I lean against the tree trunk, closing my eyes. "When will I see you?"

A pause. Muffled voices sound in the background.

"I'm hoping we'll come home for Christmas. But I can't be sure. Papa is... You know how he is."

"I know." I try to keep the disappointment from my voice. The officer's plans are out of her control.

"Today, I'm following the head nurse in pediatrics around." Her excitement breaks through. "The children are so sweet, Fred. Maybe I should major in pediatrics. Being a children's doctor might be wonderful. But I also know the importance of learning to treat everyone."

"I'm proud of you." I mean it, despite the ache in my chest. "For taking on a job caring for people. It suits you."

Someone in the background calls her name.

"I have to go," she says. "But, Fred? Please go look at the stars for me soon, okay? And when I come home, I want to see those stars with you... on our..."

My chest tightens, and I close my eyes. "I don't want to see them without you."

"Yes, you will. Promise me you'll go. God has put those stars there for us. Even when we can't see each other, we can see them and remember. I'll try to find some here too."

"I promise." The thought of sitting on our hill alone always makes me miss her so much.

"I love you," she whispers so quickly I almost miss it.

My lips part as I struggle to speak over the ball coiled in my throat. But a beep sounds on the other end. Guess I'll have to say that next time.

I stand there, phone pressed to my ear as if her voice might return. Eventually, I walk over to John, who's pacing at the end of the fence, peering over to the buildings where pupils weave in and out of classes. I return his phone and thank him.

"Everything all right?"

"She can't come." I shrug. "Her father has other plans."

He exhales, long and deep, then clamps a hand on my shoulder. "I'm sorry, son."

"I should focus and finish the task by tomorrow so I can head home."

"You're not staying until the end of the term?"

Only if Lucy were coming. "No point." I kick the cut grass, and it flies beneath my rubber flats. "My purpose here is done. I need to help my family with the harvest. Make some money before the institute starts... if I get in."

"*When* you get in," he corrects. "You've done your best, and I know you have this."

I give him a half smile and hold out my hand. "Thank you, sir. For everything."

He shakes it. "Gertrude is coming tomorrow. Don't leave before we eat lunch together."

"I won't leave without saying goodbye."

Sooner rather than later, a new day presses in. Dreading seeing my father, I cling to the thought of my mother and siblings.

By early afternoon, I've settled onto John's veranda. He leans back in his chair, Gertrude perched beside him, a lazy breeze fluttering her dress hem. We've already eaten lunch, and now we're picking at mandazi and sipping soda Gertrude brought out, the taste sweet but sitting heavy in my stomach.

"I'll miss this place, actually." My gaze drifts to the teacher quarters across the compound, neat rows of housing standing shoulder to shoulder.

"If you're bringing your sister here next year..." Gertrude's fingers curl around her orange soda bottle. Her legs swing lazily. "You'll come on visitation days."

"That's not set in stone yet."

John, seated beside me, elbows on his knees, nods like he's weighing every word. "I'll let you know as soon as I find a place for her to stay."

Hope stirs in my chest.

"We still have a long break before we have to worry about that." The lie burns my tongue. I know the fight waiting at home—to make Mama and Father believe Viola's worth more than marriage and housework.

We fall into easy small talk. Between bites of mandazi, Gertrude asks what crops I'll be bringing to the market.

Every other weekend, I've been trekking home, checking the fields, and making sure there's enough food and that the cow Lucy gave me is still healthy. So far, she's thriving, and the milk's kept my family steady.

"I'll reach out to vendors for you." Gertrude wipes her hands on a napkin. "If we manage to get some lined up, you'll need to deliver your crops early. The merchants won't wait around for latecomers."

At that, I push to my feet. "I'll leave tomorrow." I'm already calculating the route. Better to cycle it in one go than camp along the road for the night. "I need to pack up my things and clean out the house."

"We'll see you in town." Gertrude rises and brushes what must be imaginary dust from her dress.

John stands too and extends his hand. "I'm proud of you, son." His firm grip latches on, the kind you feel in your chest long after the handshake ends. "You've come further than anyone expected."

I hold on a second longer than necessary. "I don't know how I'll ever repay you."

"It's my job as headmaster to see that every student succeeds." His broad smile holds such kindness. "But if you still need work before the term starts, I'll connect you here at school for a job. The gardens always need weeds pulled."

He knows I'll need money for the institute even if I get a sponsorship. For books, clothes, and spending money.

"Thank you." I nod. "I'll visit your shop next week. The beans did well this year." I'll be bringing them some as a reward.

"Your family is lucky to have such a hardworking young man."

At her words, I choke out a laugh. "My father would disagree."

Gertrude's face falters. "Your father's one of those men who can't see what's right in front of him."

"But that's okay." John's voice hardens, his expression shadowed. "Not everyone has to understand your path for it to be the right one."

Taking comfort in John's last sentence, I cling to it as I gather my belongings and clean out the small room beneath the ceiling light's yellow glow. Yes, not everyone in the village has to understand why I'm not married, why I'm blindly believing in love, in Lucy, that someday she and I will start a family together. No one has to understand why I have to further my education so I can extend what I've learned to our village. I stack my textbooks at the bottom of the suitcase and fold my clothes neatly on top. When I lift my pillow, something shifts.

The photo album. Lucy's gift from the start of second term waits underneath, right where I'd hidden it.

Thoughts of Lucy dominate the long journey home. From the moment I stop in town at Gertrude's shop to buy mandazi, memories swamp me. The town thrums, vendors shout over one another, and children weave between stalls, the air thick with the scent of frying oil and roasted maize. And I see it all again—Lucy sitting beside me on this veranda, laughing as we share a bottle of soda and a greasy pastry.

As I cycle along the dusty road out of town, the path grows quieter, flanked by towering mango trees. Their heavy branches droop low, the ripe, golden fruit scenting the warm air. We once picnicked here, juice dripping from our chins as we peeled the sticky mango skins with our teeth. Further on, the hill rises—the same one she taught me to slide down like a child, dry grass scratching my legs, loose dirt slipping underfoot as I tumbled after her, laughing against my will.

I pedal harder, and I'm soon passing Lucy's house, the imposing mansion. A few chickens peck around the empty yard. No laundry flutters on the line. No kids chasing each other. Alex should be out of school by now. Senior four finished their exams earlier than the rest of the school, but he could still be in the city, waiting for his two sisters to finish their term. A heavy stillness sits over the place.

I keep pedaling, pushing down the urge to stop like I do to inquire about Lucy. But the bag of mandazi strapped to my bicycle is probably cold by now.

By the time I reach our land, the sky is bruised purple and orange, the colors bleeding into each other like a healing wound. And my heart shares their ache.

The path's familiar curve opens onto our compound—mud-brick huts spread apart, thin smoke drifting from cooking firepits between, the faint smell of cow dung woven into the air.

My little brother spots me first. A flash of bare feet pounds the packed earth as he barrels my way, shouting my name. "Mama! Fred is back!"

My mother emerges from her hut, wiping her hands on the colorful cloth tied around her waist. A charcoal-blackened pot bubbles over the firepit. She smiles wide, her eyes bright with warmth. "You came just in time. The potatoes are almost ready."

"I missed your cooking." I grin as I swing off the bicycle, careful to balance it against the papaya tree near her hut.

One by one, my younger siblings storm out of wherever they were playing, swarming around me. Their dusty hands grab at my shirt as they ask if I brought them some sweets.

"In a little bit." I pat their heads, and their faces glow. My one-year-old brother wobbles after a chicken with a stick, his cloth diaper slipping loose, and I can't help but smile.

"Hello, Mama." I bow low, and she lowers herself slightly to shake my hand, the edge of her wrap brushing the dusty earth.

Seeing her nearly kneel, an old habit rooted in respect, pulls at something inside me. Lucy taught me so much about equality, but that won't ever be part of the village where women are always kneeling.

I squeeze her callused fingers. "I brought some mandazi if you'd like to have some tea."

"Don't tell me you've brought city delicacies now." Her eyes atwinkle, she shakes a finger in mock disapproval.

"It's not as big a city as you think."

"I'll go get the tea started." She disappears into the hut.

I dig through the bag, paper crinkling. The warm, slightly greasy smell drifts up as I pull the package free, and the kids start jumping up and down in excitement.

"Fred!" Viola's voice breaks through the air, and she runs from my hut.

I told her that any time she needs to read, my hut is the place, and her books will be safe.

She throws her arms around me, and I do the same. Lucy taught both of us the embraces.

"Have you gotten a lot taller since I last saw you?"

"Just turned fourteen, you know."

"No way." I don't think it's actually her birthday yet, but we have to estimate ages in this village, where most kids are born at home without hospital records.

"Did you pass?" she asks.

My other siblings join in, tugging at my arms.

"What's the city like?"

"It's bigger than our village." My school wasn't in the city center. I wriggle free, then knuckle their heads.

"Did you bring biscuits?" another one pipes up, snatching the mandazi bag from my hand.

Their voices ease my earlier tension about Lucy's absence.

Mama sets out a stool for me after making tea, and we sit, drinking while she rests on the mat with my siblings, all of them enjoying their mandazi. The smell of woodsmoke and cooking food envelops me, familiar and comforting.

Mama tells me about the cow, its mischief and stubbornness whenever my half brother tries to milk it.

"At least you got some milk at all." Laughing, I ask if they've been feeding the cow well.

"At the officer's house, they feed them full-time," she says. "Not just whenever they feel like it."

"Now that you're done wasting time with books"—Father's voice cuts through it all like a machete—"you can start fixing up your house for Safiri's arrival."

"I didn't hear what you just said." I heard him, of course, but just in case, I'd better clarify. I stand, suddenly stiff.

He marches closer and stops paces away. His shirt, once red, has faded to a dull pink and looks two sizes too small for his belly. He crosses his arms, his face hard in the dying light. His nostrils flare as he drags in a breath and lets it out. "Safiri is ready. Her parents are waiting. You're not a child anymore."

My mother claps and ushers the children along. "Go eat inside."

She knows what's coming. Father and I might explode, and it's better if the little ones don't pick up my bad habits like talking back.

I square my shoulders, clench my hands tight at my sides, and step forward. "I'm not marrying her. I'm going to university." Institute or college—whichever will take me with a sponsorship. I applied to seven of them, all in a city within a twenty-minute radius of Lucy's school.

"Books have only made you more foolish." He snorts. "You still think the officer's daughter will marry you once she gets her fancy job? She's no farmer's wife." He wags a chubby finger at me. "When are you going to get it through your thick skull? That girl is wasting your time."

His words strike at my deepest fear. What if Lucy *does* find someone better? Someone who deserves her? I shove the thought down. I can't let him see that wound.

"This isn't about her." But I can't keep my pulse from hammering in my ears. "It's about my future."

"Your future." His laughter cuts deep, biting and bitter. "You can't eat dreams, boy."

My joy drains out like water through cracked hands. My appetite vanishes.

I march to the tree where my bicycle leans, and twigs crunch under my rubber sandals. I grab the bicycle and roll it past him. I hear my mother ushering the children away from the door where they're peeking out through the brown floral curtain.

Not until I reach my hut, park the bicycle, step inside, and slam the door shut, do I drag in a full breath. I set my bag on the bed and rake a hand through my short hair. I'd kept it neat at school. That life feels far away already.

CHAPTER 4

THE WORLD AWAY

Lucy

The antiseptic smell clings to my skin—the new clean scent of what my future will become. I'm eighteen now and will be nineteen before the UACE results return in late January.

I follow Nurse Juliet down the corridor, our shoes squeaking against the shiny cement floors. Her white dress complements my pink, and a metal badge declares her name and title, whereas mine has only a plastic tag with my name and no title.

We pass plastic chairs lined against the off-white walls, occupied by waiting parents bouncing fussy babies on their knees, coughing toddlers clutching worn fabric animals, and elderly men who look like they've been sitting here since the beginning of time.

Through the window, Kampala's outskirts buzz with life. Motorcycles whiz between cars, frustrated car drivers slam their horns, and street vendors call out prices. All that combines with the music from a vendor selling CDs in contrast to the beeping machines and hushed conversations about life and death inside these walls.

"Lucy, take these files to the outpatient desk. I need to see if Dr. Libya is in today." Juliet speaks without breaking stride, her voice brisk and efficient. Already three steps ahead, she moves with the confidence of someone who knows where she belongs. Her braids are pulled back tightly, not a strand out of place. I might need to style my hair the same way if the hospital becomes my life. "Then help Michael prepare the immunization cards for tomorrow's clinic."

"Yes, Nurse." I swallow my question about whether she remembers I'm only observing.

At the outpatient desk, forms are being stamped, files passed back and forth, and phones ringing. An ancient printer whirs, spitting out papers one slow sheet at a time. A line of patients waits—some slumped in plastic chairs, others hunkered on the floor against the wall, and all their faces inked with worry, pain, and exhaustion.

My heart aching, I smile at the receptionist as she finishes signing a form and hands it to a woman across the table—another receptionist, maybe. I hand the heavyset woman the brown file.

She sets the folder on the desk, obviously aware of what it contains, then glances at my badge, her eyes kind. "Observing?" At my nod, she raises a brow. "I hope you're good with paperwork. We need a lot of help today."

"It seems busy." Honestly, it's been just as busy since I got here a week ago.

"Honey, this is a slow day." She lets out a rich, rolling laugh. "You just missed the rainy season."

"Malaria is no joke." I shiver. Each rainy season, even at school, the mosquito swarms rise, and the dispensary overflows with sick kids.

With several people hovering, waiting to speak to her, she ushers me toward a back room, the records room, apparently. It's a jumble of mismatched files and cardboard boxes stacked in precarious towers against the walls. Fluorescent lights add to the glow streaming through the window. "Michael will show you what to do."

A lanky-framed guy stands bent over a table dominated with small yellow cards. He looks up and grins, revealing a slight gap between his front teeth. Though his youthful face suggests he might be in his twenties, his confident handling of the paperwork betrays more experience.

"Hello." I wave.

"I was beginning to think Juliet sacrificed you to the surgical department." He pushes his glasses up his nose. "They're always looking for fresh bodies to observe sutures."

Watching operations was what I'd hoped. "She had me running files all morning." At least it's different from the other tasks I've done since starting here.

"Ah, the glamorous life of medical interns." He winks. "But you're still far from medical school, which qualifies you for this task."

He slides a stack of blank cards toward me, then nods toward a smaller desk by the window, barely half the size of his own. A neat pile of yellow cards awaits me. "Start filling those out with tomorrow's date and the hospital stamp. We're expecting at least seven hundred children tomorrow."

Uncapping a pen, I mention the crowded corridors. "Has it always been this busy?"

"Busier during the rainy season. Mosquitoes breed, malaria spikes, and then we're playing musical beds." He shrugs. "You'll get used to it. The chaos becomes normal after a while."

"I'm not sure I'll do any serious tasks. I'm just here to observe."

"There's always work they'll give you." He stands up straight in his button-down shirt tucked into green trousers, then hands me a card to use as a sample so I know what I'm doing. It seems simple enough. He also walks me through the process of organizing the cards by date, age group, and vaccine type, showing me how to code each one for easy retrieval during the clinic rush.

I arrange the stack by age, sliding one card after another into neat piles. It isn't the glamorous task I imagined back when I dreamed of following a medical professional's footsteps.

I want to be a doctor someday. But nursing's a good first step, a way to get a feel for the hospital environment. Still, nothing about my life is unfolding the way I planned.

I should be home right now, back in the village with Mama and my siblings. Closer to Fred.

"This isn't shadowing for nursing."

"True," Michael answers without pausing in his task. "But if they are walking you through the ropes of a hospital environment for free, they have to utilize your presence. This might help you ease into different tasks." He explains how he couldn't afford nursing school, but his voluntary work earned him a sponsorship to become a CNA. "Most times, I have to go through paperwork to make sure the children aren't receiving duplicate vaccines."

"You're right. I should be grateful to get an idea of what being a nurse or doctor will be like."

"Soon, you'll get to observe surgeries. Not just for kids, you'll learn how to treat and operate on adults and children someday."

That grabs my attention. If I should ever become a doctor, especially in the village where there is no physician, treating patients of all ages will be invaluable.

We work in silence, stamping and writing. Beyond the small window, a slice of blue sky beckons, a single cloud drifting across it like a boat on still water.

After completing the cards, my fingers cramp from adding the date and stamping. At least we don't have to write all seven hundred cards. Most had been done prior.

I'm then assigned to learn to sort incoming lab results, matching them with patient files—another task more clerical than medical, but in this one, I get a glimpse into patterns of diseases and treatments.

At lunch, I sit with nursing students who've been interning longer than I have. They crowd around a table in the staff canteen, discussing medical terminology and gossiping about doctors. Some carry themselves with a hint of arrogance, speaking of patients in clinical terms that strip away humanity. Others show genuine compassion, discussing cases with concern.

I'm so relieved when I'm excused for the day.

I text my best friend, Molly, during my ten-minute taxi ride back to the barracks to let her know we can watch a movie when I get home. The place is so quiet since my brother and sister left for the village three days ago. Papa dropped them off and was back the next day, afraid I wouldn't survive left alone for many days.

My phone beeps with a text.

Molly: You'll love the new plan even better.

I smile, eager for whatever plans she has.

With my backpack slung over one shoulder, I yawn as I step into the dusty compound of police quarters. Five metal-sided offices guard the entrance. Papa is probably in his office—the larger central structure.

I could stop by and say hello, but I'd better not disturb him. I'll see him at home in a few hours anyway.

Farther down, kids from the housing across the street—all police families—run through parched patches of grass. Most of them pause, dropping their ball or stepping out from behind trees, their curious faces turning toward me.

The faded green-metal-roofed huts, some rusty, have no designated path to each home, and multiple similar units cluster together for efficiency. So our house stands out with an expansive driveway. The creamy yellow house with white trim and a red roof displays the luxury the government has offered to Papa and the officers in charge of this county zone who lived in it previously. Across from the smaller huts stands a row of four terraced houses with a uniform design. Papa's assistant—Molly's father—and the other ranked officers live there.

Molly is waiting under the tree by our driveway.

My face splits into a broad grin. "Are you *that* bored?"

She looks up from her phone, and her face lights up. "Don't let my papa hear you say that." She shoves her phone into the deep pocket of her brown skirt. She approaches with easy grace, her slender hips swaying. We're about the same height, but Molly always carries herself like she's two inches taller.

"What's the plan?" I intertwine our hands and head toward my house.

"We were waiting for you to get back." She swings our joined hands, beaming. "Hugh set us up to go swimming. Marvin's parents are out, but they said it's fine if he has friends over."

I rarely get the chance to swim with so few pools around. I free my hand and shake my index finger at her, feigning my best dorm-perfect look. "Are you sure this won't turn into one of your moments with Marvin, leaving me and Hugh to argue?"

"Promise." She crosses her heart with her now-free hand, her eyes dancing in the golden evening light. "But of course"—she gives me a knowing look—"it'll be nice to see Marvin. When else am I going to see him?"

Both our fathers are strict. Mr. Jenga isn't as strict as my papa, but being around Papa has rubbed up on him.

"Let me see if my father will be okay with that."

She nods, and I call Papa. He agrees after I confirm Molly is with me and we'll be at her friend's house—a place I assure him Mr.

Jenga knows well. Little does he know that Hugh, Molly's twin, will be with us too. Marvin's house is one of the few homes with a swimming pool, which marks them as truly wealthy in Kampala.

After the call, I change quickly. Then we head to Molly's house. Hugh is on their veranda, tossing a ball into the air and catching it again.

"You sure need a job," I tease.

He looks up, grinning. "Lucy. I'm glad you could come."

"Couldn't pass up swimming." I fan myself with my hand. The heat presses down thick and heavy.

Molly darts into the house, shouting that she's grabbing swim towels and changing into her costume.

Hugh's gaze lingers on me, and I shift my bag to the other hand, questioning the dress I threw over my swimsuit.

"What's with that look?"

"You look... different." He flashes a familiar, cocky grin as he saunters toward me. "In a good way."

He's wearing swim shorts with tiny elephant print and a faded blue T-shirt. His shoulders seem broader than I remember from the last holiday. His eyes are warm brown like Molly's, but where his sister buzzes with endless energy, Hugh moves with an easy, arrogant confidence.

"I want to hear all about school this term." He leans in for a quick hug.

With my swim bag slung over one shoulder, I manage to wrap one arm around him. "Molly said your recent girl dumped you. What did you do this—?"

"Lucy." He slaps my shoulder, his grin wide. "Clearly, you don't believe everything Molly says."

Actually, it was the other way around, but I don't feed his ego.

Hugh's handsome, the kind of guy girls trip over themselves to impress. No doubt, he'll find a holiday fling soon enough—probably not the same girl he brought around last time. Still, for all his swagger, he's a solid friend. Like a brother. One who shows up, teases you, and manages to have your back when it matters.

"Hugh!" Molly bursts back out of the house, waving a towel over her head. "Go get your swim bag! I'm not doing everything for you."

He tosses his head back and groans, letting the ball thud to the ground.

We swim at Marvin's house until dusk. The water is cool and soothing against my skin after the day's heat. Marvin's large backyard offers trimmed grass and potted plants along the brick fence, and the pool itself glints like glass under the fading sun. His parents and two younger siblings have gone to inspect a boarding school in the western part of the country where his sister might start primary one next term. The caretaker stayed behind to watch the house.

We toss a ball back and forth in the water and drift into conversations about university plans. Molly wants to become a teacher, and Hugh's aiming for business. They hope to find an affordable institute offering both programs so they can attend together.

"Do you know where you're going yet, Molly?" Marvin's eyes soften toward her as I throw the ball her way.

"We're not sure just yet." She tosses him the ball with a splash of water. "Wherever we end up, we probably won't stay on campus."

"That works for me." Hugh catches the ball from Marvin.

Marvin plans to study law. He's already been accepted to Uganda's most prestigious university. Of course, he has. He's medium height, with the calm confidence of someone you want to listen to. I can picture him in a suit and tie, standing in a courtroom, arguing cases with that steady voice and composed presence.

We talk about random things too—the twins' upcoming visit to their mother in January, how quiet the barracks will be once they leave. Hugh wants to know how my term went. So I tell him about training the new dorm prefect, losing the dorm keys, and accidentally getting the matron in trouble with the headmistress for giving the keys to a student. Hugh and Molly share about their school too—how their head girl fainted during the parade from standing too long and how Hugh spent his last week before final exams working in the field for missing morning prep.

"That's the one thing I'd cut out of the school routine. Even adults can't wake up at four a.m., why make us do that?" Hugh smirks. "I told the teacher I'd skip morning prep all over if I was still in high school."

"As long as they keep football, I'm happy." Marvin mimics a kick underwater. "Our team finally won a match after months of losing."

"Nice going." Hugh splashes him, and Molly beams while the boys wrestle in the water.

"Football might've been nothing to brag about." Marvin smirks as he shoves Hugh away. "The real challenge? *I* got picked to lead prayers during the final assembly because the teacher thought I looked responsible. Me!"

He does, of course, but we don't say it.

The sun dips as we laugh, joke, and float in the water. Through it all, Marvin looks at Molly with that soft kind of admiration, and she laughs at everything he says, even when it's not all that funny. They started noticing each other near the end of last term's holiday—almost a year ago now. But since they won't be going to the same university, their relationship feels as uncertain as mine and Fred's.

As the sun sinks lower, painting the sky in streaks of orange and violet, we gather near the veranda to eat supper. The caretaker made matooke, rice, and beef stew—served with stainless steel cutlery and tall juice glasses.

They eat like kings here. Even though I'm considered well-off by some standards, we don't eat meat on a random weekday. Not just for friends. Not without parents around.

We settle in to watch an American action film on the enormous television. The living room is spacious and modern with plush leather sofas and bright-colored art splashed across the walls—a world away from the barracks homes.

"I'll sit next to Lucy." Hugh drops down beside me, and his shorts brush against my dress.

It makes sense so his sister and Marvin can get better acquainted.

With the movie full of suspense, people jumping off buildings, and heart-pounding music, it's hard to look away. Then my phone rings, cutting through the TV. I glance at the screen. It's Gertrude's community line—the one she uses for her shop.

My stomach dips, and excitement flickers up into my chest. No way Fred would still be in town this late, right? I check the time. Nine thirty.

"Don't tell me it's Farm Boy." Hugh's breath warms my cheek.

I hadn't realized how close he'd leaned until I looked up. Too close.

Fred. Unless it's just Gertrude.

"Go answer before it hangs up." Molly urges me toward the front door.

I hurry out onto the veranda. My heart thumps. My voice emerges too breathy. "Hello?"

"Lucy." Fred breathes my name like it's something delicate, something he's missed.

And just like that, I feel light—as if I could float like popcorn in oil.

"Fred." Longing to be near him floods through me. I move further onto the veranda, the cement cool beneath my bare feet. "What are you still doing in town this late?"

"I thought maybe if I called you at night, I'd get ahold of you. How's the hospital learning going?"

Smiling, I lean against the brick wall. Moths dance around the outdoor light. "They haven't made me a doctor yet. Just a glorified file clerk." I tell him about the various tasks I've done so far. "Papa bought me lots of medical books. I'll be learning a lot."

"But you sound good." Something like resignation ladens his voice. "You sound... happy."

The statement hangs between us, like a question he's too afraid to ask. *Are you happier there, without me?*

"I miss home." Which means him, since the village never really was my home. Does he understand that I want to reassure him he's a part of my home? "Have you stopped by to see Mama?"

"I've been stopping by this week. Seeing your siblings and your mama always makes me feel closer to you."

I take a deep breath. "I miss you."

Silence stretches between us, filled with all the things we haven't said.

"I think about you every day," he says. "The photos you gave me help me to see your face when I miss you most."

An ache settles in my chest. If only I could call him whenever I wanted. "Tell me something good. About home, about you, your siblings, Viola..."

"Stargazing's been a must." He then tells me about his daily life. Hard work under the unforgiving sun as he provides for his family. He talks about the cow I gave him, how it delivered a calf, which eventually means more milk for the children in his family. "Lots of tilling the soil. I'll be bringing more produce to sell in town soon."

I picture him sitting under a sprawling mango tree on a hot day, taking a brief respite from cultivating the land. Surely, I can handle my work at the hospital if Fred works six times harder without complaint.

"I've been using your songs to teach Viola." His voice warms. "If John finds a place for her to stay, I want her to go to school too."

My chest tightens. I want the same for his siblings and all the children in the village. "I think we can make sure of it." I'm willing to pay if I can find money so his sister can go to school.

"Viola thinks you like me too much since you made those learning songs just for me."

I laugh, remembering the silly melodies I created to help him memorize facts for his exams. "And what do you think?"

He laughs too, and the sound makes my chest ache with longing. "She's right. I like you even more."

I glance back through the window. The others are engrossed in the film, laughing at something I can't hear.

Hugh then turns, and his gaze drifts to the window where I'm standing.

"I'm so glad you called." But while he's talking to me now, he's accumulating a bill for the call. Money he needs to save for his school. "I love you, Fred."

He breathes through the phone. "I love you more."

Instead of hanging up, I wait, wanting to cherish each moment, just listening to his breathing.

Then he asks, "Will you come home for Christmas?"

I pause, hand on the door. Back to the village, to Fred, to our hill beneath the stars?

"I don't think so." I'm still hoping Papa was just toying with the idea he told me two days ago. "Papa wants us to celebrate Christmas at our home in Mukono."

I wasn't pleased at all, but his surprise plans made sense because we could celebrate with Grandmother—Mom's mother who lives closer to our city home. Dad had said, "Your mother has been heartsick since Cutie died."

"Oh, Lucy." Fred's voice sounds like a deflated balloon. "I feel like—"

"I'll find a way to see you, Fred. I will."

When we hang up, I press the phone to my chest as if I can somehow hold the conversation there, keep it close to my heart. I'm not ready to go back inside. I need to savor this moment.

Then Hugh calls through the half-open window. "Lucy, you're going to miss the good part."

They've paused the movie now. They're all leaning back, waiting.

I step back into the blurry living room, leaving the night—and Fred—behind. This is my reality for now. One where Fred and I can't see each other even as we hold each other dear.

CHAPTER 5

THE WEEK BEFORE CHRISTMAS

Fred

The December sun is brutal. It blazes like it's got something to prove, hammering down until sweat beads on my forehead, then spills in slow streams down my temples and spine. I swing my leg over the bicycle and lean it against a wooden canteen, breath short.

My shirt clings to my back, and my fingers ache as I untie the sacks. First, the beans. I ease them to the ground, careful not to let the twine snap. Then I shift the sack of sweet potatoes off one side of the bike's levered bar and the cassava from the other. Balancing the weight on either side worked for the thirty-five-kilometer ride, but the hills still left my legs feeling like jelly.

I tried to get here early to beat the crowds. But from the look of the open stalls and vendors and merchants already calling out prices, it must be past nine.

Too late.

Other farmers and older women—both seasoned—are already making trades, their voices rising with bartering. I sling the sack of beans over my shoulder and grab the sweet potatoes. I'll come back for the cassava if someone's interested.

As I pass a food stall, the smell of fried mandazi punches me in the gut. Hunger twists my stomach, but even more, the smell stirs memories of being here with Lucy. It was the first time I'd tested soda and samosa. We can never afford oil to fry anything.

She smiled the whole time, talking about the Nile and dreaming about me seeing it, rather than just reading about it in Geography. The day she made those dreams real feels like a lifetime ago.

Now, this Christmas, I won't see her. Not even for five minutes like last year.

I shake the thought off and step behind a scruffy-bearded man trading eggs. The vendor greets him with easy familiarity. They count coins, laugh at something I miss, then shake hands. On my turn, I clear my throat and set the sack down.

"Hello." I force my voice steady. "I'm Fred. Gertrude said you might be interested in beans."

The man barely looks up. "You're late. Already bought some for the week."

I glance at his stand. Potatoes running low. "Would you be needing potatoes?"

"Delivered already. After Christmas, maybe. But be here by eight next time."

I nod, trying to hide the burn of frustration behind my teeth. "Thank you, sir."

I move on. Another stand. Then another. All say the same thing. One needs some cassava. Not much.

I whisper a silent prayer like Lucy's mom would've told us to do.

At the next stand, a woman is arranging her potatoes. Her husband adjusts the scale behind her. She shakes her head at my offer of beans. "We're not buying much until after Christmas. We have to get some Christmas gifts for the kids."

Her husband glances up. "Did you say you've got potatoes?"

Hope flares. "Yes, sir. I'll give you a good bargain too."

He squints at me like he's testing my sincerity. But he nods.

In the end, he buys three extra kilos of beans too, on one condition—a better price. I throw in some cassava at a bargain, and he agrees.

It's the first time I've sold anything but the corn I sell at the mill. And Gertrude was right—having variety earns me profit. The quicker I sell, the sooner I pay for school. I'm still holding out for a sponsorship. But if I don't get one, I need backup.

After I've sold what I can, I haul the rest to Gertrude's shop. I owe her, especially after the long phone call she let me make to Lucy last week.

She's in the back, stacking fabric by color.

"Look who finally returns." She dusts off her hands on her apron, eyes twinkling. "You sell it all or just give it away for free?"

"Didn't help that I was late." I shake my head. "One man made me lower my price like five times."

"Welcome to the market." She jerks her chin toward the counter. "What did you bring back?"

"Cassava and a few potatoes." I lift the sacks in my hands. "One woman said I can come back tomorrow, but she wasn't sure."

Gertrude walks around the long table, takes the sack from me, and peeks inside. "Looks fresh. I'll buy the rest."

"I still owe you for the call."

"Let's call it even with this." She smiles kindly. "Or Lucy will pay when she returns to buy me a whole crate of soda, like she promised on the phone."

I take off my hat, the one Lucy gave me, and the words catch in my throat. "You already know she's not coming this Christmas."

Gertrude tilts her head to the side, sympathy in her eyes. "I know."

The silence stretches between us. Then she hefts the sacks. "I'll put these in the back. While here, you may as well call her."

And I do, but I don't get a hold of her.

When Gertrude returns, she must sense I didn't get through. She presses her lips tight. I say goodbye, but she stops me with a hand on my arm. "Fred, it's all going to be fine."

I nod, grateful Gertrude and John support my relationship with Lucy—too bad, they're the only adults who do. It's nice to have them in my life. I struggle to speak past the lump in my throat. "I'll be back next market day."

She nods, and a burn of embarrassment tingles my neck over acting weak and hopeless.

The sun's still climbing, glaring hot and golden, when I reach Primrose, Lucy's mother's compound. One glance at the truck parked outside, and my blood surges.

Lucy's father is here.

My chest tightens. Could Lucy be here too? She said she wouldn't come, but maybe she did.

I slow down, climb off my bike, and push it along, careful not to rattle the dry weeds lining their property. Wildflowers blur my vision as I scan the compound, eyes locked on the wide veranda before their massive house. I don't see anyone, but my stomach's already in knots.

Even if Lucy's not here, her father—the officer—definitely is. And the last thing I need is for him to spot me skulking on his property. He made his opinion of me clear the day he exchanged bitter words with my father. That conversation still rings in my ears.

I drag the bike behind a clump of bushes near the forest line, hiding it beneath the low branches. My shoulders sag even without the weight of produce. The dirt's soft beneath my rubber sandals as I crouch under the shade, letting the breeze brush the sweat off my neck.

I wait.

A child's laugh snaps my head up.

Then footsteps.

Through the brush, I spot Alex out in the compound, showing his younger siblings how to use some complicated-looking toy—probably something their father brought back from the city. It spins and lights up, catching the kids' squeals like fireflies in a jar.

I let myself smile. If I call out now, they'll scream my name, and their father will storm out like a lion chasing prey. I shift, and a dry twig cracks underfoot.

Alex looks up. His gaze sweeps the trees, then lands on me. When I lift a hand to wave, he grins like he's been expecting me all along.

Of course, he has.

He sends the kids inside and strides toward me. He's taller now—leaner, more grown. Must be seventeen now, four years older than Viola. He used to be our go-between, sneaking letters and messages when Lucy's father tightened the leash.

He doesn't ask why I'm hiding in the shadows. He already knows.

But then he retrieves something from his shorts' large side pocket. "Lucy sent these for you in the package she sent with Papa. I had to open it since it was addressed to me." He shrugs. "Until I read the letter inside."

"Binoculars." I start to look at them when he hands me a pink envelope with my name written across it—Lucy's handwriting. My hand shakes as I take it. I swallow hard at the urge to be alone when I read whatever she sent me.

"I've been thinking," Alex says as my index finger traces my name on the envelope. "Anyway." He glances over his shoulder, checking to make sure the coast is clear. I move deeper into the trees, and he follows. "I need a new and advanced slingshot."

I raise a brow. "And how are you planning to get that?"

He smirks. "Next time you want news about Lucy, I expect payment in the form of high-quality weapons."

"You sound like a criminal."

"Just an entrepreneur." But then his face sobers. "Were you hoping she'd be here?"

My throat tightens, and I nod.

His gaze drops, and the toe of his sandal scuffles a leaf at our feet. "Papa's here to take us to the city for Christmas."

My heart stumbles. "When are you leaving? How long will you stay in the city? Are you coming back? Is Lucy—"

"I don't know how long." He holds up a hand. "Maybe a few weeks. Mama's been having a hard time since Cutie died. She doesn't feel like the village is home anymore."

I understand. Still, a cold tingling dread climbs my spine. If they all move to the city permanently, I may never see Lucy again. Unless I somehow get that sponsorship and move too.

But even if I do, who takes care of my siblings? Who helps Viola with her reading? Who helps Mama with the fields?

I'm pulled in two directions, and neither one feels right.

"We leave tomorrow," Alex adds. "Early."

I exhale shakily. "Can you meet me tonight? At the creek?"

He tilts his head. "You're giving me a slingshot already?"

"No." I smile despite myself. "Something for Lucy."

He nods, this time without teasing. "Let's meet after supper."

I retrieve my bike and continue on my way. When I get home, I don't expect to see anyone outside, let alone Viola, sitting under the mango tree by my hut.

She's hunched forward in the shade, her back straight, fingers working in rhythm like the world depends on what she's doing. The tangy scent of crushed leaves and ripe mangoes hangs in the air. Chickens scratch at scattered grain in the compound, and long shadows stretch across the packed earth.

I lean my bicycle against the hut, my muscles still sore from the ride. The crunch of twigs underfoot gives me away.

Viola's head lifts. Her eyes sparkle, and something in my chest eases just seeing her smile. "Fred, you're back."

I walk over and lower myself beside her, wincing as twigs jab at my hand. She's threading colorful beads onto a string, a half-finished bracelet coiled near her lap.

"What are you making?"

"A bracelet. To sell at the market. I want to help you raise money for your school faster."

My heart twists, and my eyes blur as her small hands move. She's only fourteen but carries herself like someone older, heavier with responsibility. No wonder my parents might think she'll be ready for marriage next year—shutting down her dreams before she even has a chance.

She's a fast learner. Lucy must've shown her how to bead once and left her with supplies. Viola's ambition burns quietly, stubbornly.

And it hits me—how much of that quiet fire comes from Lucy. The beads. The books. The whispered encouragement when no one else was paying attention.

"You've gotten good at that."

"Lucy is a good teacher."

"What if I pay you for that one?" I finger the bracelet, careful not to pull it loose. It's beautiful, yellow, blue, and red. Lucy's bright colors. I'll send it with Alex when he goes to the city.

Viola glances up, eyes curious, innocent. "What am I supposed to tell Mama about where I got the money?"

"You don't tell her anything." I lower my voice. "In fact… I've been thinking. When the new term starts, you should be in school too." Of course, once sleeping arrangements are worked out.

She pauses, beads clutched between her thumb and forefinger. "Father says I need to start preparing for matrimony next year."

The word *matrimony* lands like a slap.

I sit up straighter, heat crawling up my neck. "Matrimony to who?"

She looks away. "He thinks Solomon might be ready for a new wife."

Solomon. That old man treats his cows better than people. My jaw clenches so tight it aches.

"He'll be sorry if he steps anywhere near you." My fists curl so hard my knuckles crack. Heat surges through my arms, my body bracing like I'm ready for a fight. "That's not happening."

My voice comes out too sharp, too loud. Birds explode from the nearby tree, wings beating the air in frantic bursts.

"I don't care what Father says."

Viola flinches, shrinking back. "I can't talk to him like that… like you do."

"You don't have to." I drag my voice down low, forcing the rage back into my chest. "You're coming with me to the market after Christmas. I'll introduce you to Headmaster Lugire."

I've already spoken to him about her—told him how bright she is, how fast she reads, how Lucy gave her books, and how she reads better than most girls in the village do, even older ones. I'm willing to put her in the dormitory.

But that kind of plan requires money. Which I still don't have. Which means I have to keep selling like my future depends on it.

Because it does. Hers too.

"For now." Viola holds the bracelet up to the light. "I'll enjoy this one before Mama finds out I still have these beads."

I grin. "Where have you been hiding them?"

"Under your bed." She winks. "You never look under there, it seems."

I laugh, then exhale. "I want to send Lucy that bracelet."

Her eyes widen. "Is she coming for Christmas?"

The words snag in my throat. "No. Not this time."

Her smile falters, and she looks down again. "But maybe after Christmas, she'll come back."

"Maybe." I force the word out, though it sounds hollow. Lucy's job in the city keeps her busy. Her letters are fewer. Her voice is softer on the phone, like she's always about to say goodbye.

"Don't tell anyone about school," I whisper. "Not yet."

"If it happens"—she rolls the beads between her fingers. "I'll do what Lucy would do."

I raise an eyebrow. "And what's that?"

Mischief curves her grin, crinkles the edges of her eyes. "Do what's right for me and perhaps run. Not tell anyone I'm leaving."

I shake my head, laughing. "You've been around Lucy too long."

"She gave me more than books." She starts tying off the bracelet. There must be so many other girls in this village who dream like she does but never get the chance to go anywhere. Her head jerks up, eyes sharp. "Fred... when you love someone, like the way you do Lucy, how do you know when to let them go and when to fight harder?"

The question lands deep. I blink at her. Caught off guard, I open my mouth.

But I don't have the answer. Not yet.

CHAPTER 6

THE UNEXPECTED NEWS

Fred

Christmas arrives, and so does the kind of heat that makes the air taste like rust. It presses into your skin, clings to the back of your neck, crawls beneath your shirt until you're soaked through. Even the church's tin roof can't hold back the blaze—it radiates like a skillet over our heads. The cracked floor breathes up dust with every shuffle of a foot. I sneeze into my elbow more than once, trying not to miss a note as I pluck the harp strings.

Voices rise like a tide as the congregation sings, some off-key, others in tune and reflective. My fingers move through the familiar chords, muscle memory guiding them while I reflect on the words about Jesus's birth in a manger. The song stretches long, and my mind wanders. I hear Lucy through the music, even as we switch to another song. She's more present during the hymns she loved.

When the reverend starts teaching, I glance at where she would sit. I used to sneak glances during the teaching. She'd catch me, her lips curling in that smile that made my pulse misbehave. Now, a different family crowds her place.

I'm not sure how much of the reverend's teaching I grasp. But I hear him call us to our feet and instruct us to sing the hymn, "A Closer Walk with You."

At home, the compound carries its own rhythm. Father joins us for lunch before he'll head off again—to which hut, which of his other two wives, I don't know. Maybe even he doesn't.

Above me, the tree's wide-leafed branches sag under the weight of mangoes in different stages of ripening. A breeze slips through, wafting the smell of the ripe fruit and the stew Mama's been simmering all morning. Father and I perch on stools I carved from old timber, the table between us low and uneven, legs still rough with bark. Mama and the kids sit nearby on a woven mat, their legs tucked beneath them.

"Mama, you made quite a feast." I soak rice into the stew. The broth is thick and golden brown, steam curling up with the smell of garlic and dried spices.

"Your ma is a good cook." Father lifts the gizzard to his lips—the piece reserved for the head of the house. His gaze flicks toward me, almost a cue. I don't need to hear the rest to know what he's thinking. *You'll need a wife soon to cook like this.*

Mama smiles, her brown silk gown folded at her ankles, the same one she wears every Christmas, still pristine despite the years.

My younger siblings bicker over whose meat is whose. I tear mine into smaller pieces and hand them out. Across the compound, the chickens cluck and squawk, pecking at the drying corn we laid out this morning. I should shoo them off, but it's Christmas. They, too, should feast.

"Are you meeting with Faluk tomorrow?" Mama asks Father.

He leans back, his laugh deep. "His new secondhand bicycle fell apart on the road. I can just picture him, standing there holding up the pieces."

I don't find it funny, but since he didn't get hurt, I laugh because of my father's infectious laughter.

"His new... his bride..." He speaks through laughter, slapping my shoulder, unable to finish whatever he's trying to say. When laughter subsides, he extends his leftover piece of meat and slides it onto my plate in a rare act of affection.

Maybe things between us will be just fine. But then Mama leaves to wash the dishes, and the kids scatter off.

"You've finished your exams." His cream kanzu shifts as he straightens. "What now?"

I knew this was coming. I breathe slowly. "If my results are good, I should get a sponsorship at an institute."

"What do you mean, institute?" His frown deepens the unfriendly creases on his face. "Like a university?"

"It's similar." I kept the details of the less competition for sponsorships in institutes to myself. He doesn't care about logistics.

His jaw tightens. "And who will farm this land while you're off chasing books? How will you pay the bride price? Your mother was pregnant with you, by the time she was your age."

"I want to teach." My voice flat now, I fold my arms to my chest. I haven't thought through how the fields will get weeded when I can't come back every weekend. "That's still my plan."

He looks away, lips pressed into a thin line. "You keep saying that like it's enough."

What can I say? Silence hangs between us like smoke with nowhere to go. I'm grateful for the kids' happy shouts as they race each other in the shrubbery edging our homestead.

I stand to leave, but so does Father, marching across the compound toward one of the other two huts where smoke curls into the air above a saucepan set over the fire.

I join Mama at the wooden stand where dishes are drying. Bending down, I pull the basket from underneath and start stacking the clean dishes inside.

She takes a plastic cup from my hand before I can place it in the basket. "You shouldn't be doing women's work."

"It's only fair I help after you cooked for us." Lucy showed me that helping around the home doesn't make me less of a man—it's an act of love, a way to contribute to the family.

Mama tips her head to the side, her mouth tilting downward. "I'm worried about you."

"Why? Because of what Father thinks?"

"That girl is making you soft."

I blow out a breath and reach for another cup.

"Maybe you should listen to your father—"

"Mama, I don't need another lecture." The words snap out harder than I mean. I don't want to be disrespectful, not at Christmas, but I can only take so much.

She lets out a sigh, weary and sad, and my gut twists up.

"Sorry." Out of respect, it's all I can say. I keep stacking the dishes.

After a long moment, she nods and lets me be.

When I march into my hut, Viola's sprawled across my bed. The grass rooftop and clay walls keep the heat out, leaving the room cool and still. She kicks her feet lazily in the air, a book open in her hands.

"You're making yourself a little too comfortable."

She folds a dry twig into the book as a makeshift bookmark and sits cross-legged on my blanket. "What did Papa say?"

"The usual." I leave it at that. No point dragging her into the weight I'm carrying, not when she has to go back to school soon.

"Don't let me stop you from reading." I lower myself to the floor to pull out my suitcase. I unlock it with a key. Everything important to me—Lucy's letters, the small gifts she's given me—is tucked inside.

Fatigue drags at my bones, frustration eating away what little strength I have left.

"Want to play teppo?" Viola asks.

I blink. "Now?"

She grins and hops off the bed. "I'll go get the others."

She knows I could use a distraction. More than willing, I follow her outside as she races off to round up our siblings.

I draw a circle in the dirt and divide it into four sections. Our youngest sibling is too little to understand the game—or learn the names of countries—but no one seems to mind.

My heart lifts as we take turns shouting the names, despite the heat drenching my forehead and soaking through my shirt. Oops. I never changed out of my church clothes, but I don't care.

We laugh. They chase each other, barefoot and loud, stirring up dust, and the heaviness pressing against my chest eases.

When Mama calls us for supper, I just shake my head. Still too full.

My hut is darker now, shadows stretching across the dirt floor. I light the kerosene lamp. It flickers on the rickety table, casting a shaky glow against the mud walls. My mat lies folded in the corner beside the table.

At last, I pull the letter from my suitcase, needing Lucy, craving her presence like air. I unfold it, though by now, the paper is soft, the edges curled and worn, creased from being opened and closed more times than I can count.

Her words comfort me—and cut deep. They remind me why I'm still pushing through this. And how far away she really is.

Dear Fred, Christmas in the city this year won't feel like last Christmas. I miss the quiet. I miss the village. I miss your voice. But our memories while we were together hold you close to me. Don't work too hard.

I'm plotting a way to convince Papa I need to come to the village. I'm hopeful I'll see you soon. In the meantime, maybe you can use these binoculars for the stars whenever you don't feel like taking a telescope with you.

I love you so much. Love, Lucy

I trudge along the next day, working through my usual tasks, thinking of her with every step. Even as I pedal back from the well with three jerricans balanced on the bicycle—two tied to either side, one wobbling on the back seat—she's there in my mind.

My T-shirt clings to my back, damp with sweat, but the cap, Lucy's gift, shades my face from the brutal heat.

The road crunches under my tires, dry and brittle with loose stones—the kind that slip out from under you if you're not careful, threatening to send the whole load tumbling.

When I round the bend into the compound, my father's lounging under the mango tree. His white kanzu reflects the sunlight, stark against the patchy shade. Two village elders sit with him, their walking sticks leaning against their stools, heads angled in conversation.

I slow and step off my bicycle. Once they see me, their talk dies.

"Good afternoon." I nod, trying to sound neutral as I roll my bicycle past.

"Fred," Father orders, "join us."

It seems urgent, so I drag my bicycle over. I'll have to take the water to Mama's hut later. The jerricans slosh as I lean the bicycle against the tree and set them down. Sweat slicks my palms now, though not from work. Ugh. I'd rather till a stony field from dawn to dusk than sit in a circle like this. Nothing good ever follows when elders arrive without notice—especially when an empty stool's already waiting for me.

Of course, it's all planned. I lower myself onto the stool, the wood warm beneath me, sunbaked and splintering at the edges.

"We were discussing your future." The thinner elder speaks in a voice dry like papyrus. "If you are to take over your father's legacy, you must start building your household. A man needs children. And to have children—"

"I need a wife." I finish his sentence for him, the words like dust in my mouth.

"Exactly." He nods, reaches for his walking stick, and anchors it in front of him as if he needs to lean in for emphasis. His graying brows knit together. "Your father says you've finished your exams."

"I'm waiting for the results. Yes."

He nods once again, slow. "That's good." He wags a finger. "But education means nothing without responsibility."

"They've come to speak about Safiri." Father leans forward, elbows on knees, voice heavy. "Her family is growing impatient. You know the law."

"I know the law," I snap, my teeth grinding. As the oldest remaining son, I'm supposed to marry my brother's widow. "And I've already told you I want to teach." And Safiri, or any woman who isn't Lucy, isn't part of that plan.

"Enough with this foolish dream!" Father slices his hand through the air. "You need to continue the legacy. You need a wife. Soon."

"Safiri is a good girl." The short elder offers a rehearsed smile. "Her father will give you land. It's a wise match."

A breeze cuts through the tree, lifting the scent of dust and jackfruit from the nearby grove. I ground myself in it, then breathe deep.

"With all due respect," I speak slowly, evenly, "I can't marry someone I don't love."

My father's face hardens like sunbaked clay. "Love? What foolishness has the officer's daughter put in your head? Do you still see her?"

"She didn't put anything in my head." I don't need to answer whether I see Lucy or not. "I made my own choice."

"Marriage isn't about dreams." Father's words land with the finality of a verdict. "It's about building roots. Children carry your name."

"I am building something." I sit taller. "A future where Viola won't be married off at fifteen. Where my siblings—and other children in this village—can know what's beyond this field. What's possible."

The elders exchange glances. One clears his throat. "Perhaps... we'll give your family more time to discuss."

They rise, brush off their robes, and disappear down the dusty footpath between the shrubbery, their rubber sandals dragging broken twigs in their wake.

Father stands. Arms crossed, nostrils flaring, he turns on me. "You shamed me in front of the elders."

"Was I supposed to stay silent while you decided my future?" I stand and square my shoulders despite how inferior he tries to make me feel. I'm a year older than last year, nineteen.

He steps closer, voice low and trembling with rage. "You think you're better than me?"

"I think I've been given a chance." I hold my ground. "And I want to make something of it. Can you give me that?"

"You think you're different from everyone else in this village?" He snorts, fury radiating off him. "Go, then. Chase that officer's daughter and see where she gets you. But don't forget who dug these fields before you. I'm still in charge. You're my son. And if you're foolish, I'll step in."

He walks away without another word, sandals scuffing the earth, the hem of his robe catching in the breeze. His back is stiff—maybe from pride, maybe from hurt.

Step in? What does he think he's been doing this whole time?

I remain under the tree, now realizing I have fists curled at my sides. The sun has climbed higher, its heat sharp on my face. Chickens dart across the yard, flapping and pecking at the cracked ground. I admire their carefree living. I don't even swat off the bee as it buzzes against my ear. It's the least of my problems.

As I drag my bicycle across the compound, Mama steps out from the hut, shaking dust from a fiber mat. She watches her husband disappear toward his other wife's hut. No doubt, she won't see him again this week. All because of me.

CHAPTER 7

THE INTRUDER

Fred

On the day after New Year's, I return from tilling the fields, the hoe still slung over my shoulder. The morning sun has already hardened into a dry, relentless heat now sticking in my throat. My arms ache, shirt plastered to my back, and my mind's only on having cool water from the clay pot in my hut.

I blink, halting when a floral curtain sways in my door. My hut is open, and what's with the curtain?

I stop dead in the middle of the compound as if I've walked toward the wrong hut. But no—the slingshot basket is still hanging where I left it, its rope frayed. The torn rubber sandals I meant to mend this afternoon are there below the step.

This is my home. Odd, there's a curtain. Viola or Mama wouldn't put it there. They know I take care of myself.

My feet quicken, and I drop the hoe to my veranda. Then I shove the curtain aside.

And freeze. There's a woman inside.

She's folding my blanket, tucking it in like she owns the corners.

My water pot's been moved. My sandals lined up like soldiers beside the door. She's wearing a fluttery dress, not the usual gomesi that married women wear, but she's on a mission, no doubt.

Her bare feet sink into the dusty floor as she moves along the bed, smoothing the blanket, setting up camp—and claiming it.

"Safiri?"

She turns.

And heat surges up my chest. Not from desire. From betrayal. From shock. From rage.

"What are you doing here?"

She kneels.

Like a wife.

Not mine. Never mine. Lucy taught me better. Clearly her kind of kneeling isn't love—it's submission dressed as duty. It's silence forced into softness.

Her smile is gentle. Her wrapper is vibrant, and her hair is stretched smooth like she recently got a perm. It looks longer than the short hair she had at Christmas—not that I was paying attention, but my friend Henry mentioned her in passing as a joke.

"Your father said I could move in." She blinks up at me from her knees. "He said... the wedding is coming up. When you're ready."

My fists clench at my sides. Dust clings to my sweat-slicked palms like guilt.

So this is my father's strategy now. No elders. No warnings. Just move her in. Like planting a seed and expecting me to water it.

"There is no wedding." I step inside fully. My voice sharpens. "And this—" I sweep a hand across the room, ignoring the smell of fresh passion juice coming from the glass cup. Where did she even get a glass cup? "This is my home. You need to leave."

Her smile wavers, lips faltering. "But... your father assured my parents—"

"He doesn't speak for me."

Her chin lowers. How I hate the way this feels. I hate being the storm she didn't expect. A widow with no home, no voice, being handed off like a parcel.

I puff out a breath. "Please stand." This whole thing feels off. I soften my voice. "You deserve someone who chooses you. Who sees you. Not someone forced into it."

She straightens, wounded pride glinting in her eyes. "What does Lucy have that I don't?"

Please don't cry.

"My heart." The words come out freely. "It's already hers."

She gasps as if the words wounded her.

"If you gave me a chance," she whispers, "you'd grow to love me."

I say nothing. Because anything I say now will undo her.

I turn for the door.

"I made you some juice."

"I don't want it." So parched, I desperately need it, but I can't give her the wrong impression.

"I'm not leaving." She scrambles to her feet as I exit the door. "You could learn to love me. Like Lucy. You could marry two wives. Like everyone else."

I pause in the doorway, one step already out. Hot fury ignites in my chest. My hands twitch, though I'm not sure what I expect to do with them. Maybe I look terrifying because she flinches and steps back. Shame hits me harder than anything my father could throw.

I run both hands through my hair, gripping the dampness of it. "If you're not leaving, then you'll have to stay here—alone."

I storm out. My feet pound the parched compound, and dust flares at my heels. Chickens scatter, squawking. The cow lowing from the far fence stirs the familiarity I need.

Lucy's cow.

Her gift to me and my family.

And now they want to trade it all—for what? A silent agreement. A forced future.

I make for my stepmother's hut—Father's favorite place to be when he's home. The mango tree nearby casts long, crooked shadows now, and smoke curls from the charcoal stove beside the wall.

Laughter echoes behind the tree. Good. He's around. Then I see him. Squatting beside the younger boys, carving a stick—not for walking since he doesn't need aid.

"You can't use a knife yet," he tells the toddler, smiling.

"Can I use the stick to hunt, then?" another child pipes in.

A flicker of something twists in my chest. Warmth. Then grief. He gives them his time. My siblings and I never get this much tenderness from him.

"Fred!" The littlest one spots me and races across the yard. When I crouch and catch him midleap, he wraps his arms around my neck and rests his cheek on my shoulder like he doesn't want to let go. "Can I hunt with you soon? Father is making a stick."

"You'll be hunting sooner than you think." I ruffle his tight hair.

Another sibling trails him, hopeful eyes wide.

"Can you please fetch me a cup of water?" I ask. "And maybe some leftover cassava?"

They take off, eager to please.

I don't need food. Or water. Anger has replaced any thirst or hunger.

I need the truth.

I step closer. "Why?" My voice rises. "Why would you send someone into my hut without telling me?"

He barely glances at me as he shaves another sliver from the stick. "It was time to act. You've had your fun. Now you need to become a man."

My muscles tighten until I must be stiffer than the stick in his hand. "I'm not marrying Safiri. Not now. Not ever."

He chuckles. "Time will change your mind. Or hunger will."

My fists curl again. "What do you mean?"

His hand stills. He finally looks up. "No son of mine wastes his life chasing useless books. Especially not for a girl who'll never set foot in our home."

"Lucy has never—"

"Her family will always see you as less." He spits to the side. "You think her father wants his daughter with a farmer's son? Rubber sandals, dirt-stained fingers, no title?"

The words strike a part of me I keep buried.

Because I've thought about them too. But I can't flinch. "That's for me and Lucy to figure out. Not you."

I turn before he can speak again. The knife might still be in his hand, but I've taken the blade out of his control.

My bike carries me faster than my thoughts. Faster than the weight pressing against my ribs. I've probably never cycled as fast as I do now. I don't keep track of time, but I'm at Gertrude's shop before I know it.

It's another day the phone isn't in use. She mustn't make much money from other callers like she does from me, since I always find the phone available. I grip the phone tight to one ear, then hold my other hand to my other ear to keep out the noise from shouting vendors and honking taxis outside.

One ring.

Oh, God, please let Lucy answer the phone. I can't go home without reaching her today. I just can't.

Two.

Three.

"Hello?"

Her voice pours through the receiver like rain on dry soil. Familiar. Steady. Everything I forgot I needed.

"Lucy."

"Fred?" Her breath catches. "I—I dreamed about you last night. I kept the phone close, hoping you'd call. I even called the shop earlier."

Tears burn my eyes. She sensed my internal struggle even from afar. She sure is meant to be mine.

"I..." My voice trembles. How do I even begin?

"Is everything okay?"

I breathe hard. My voice comes out like gravel. "Safiri moved into my hut."

A long pause comes between us. Did she hang up?

Then she gulps. "What?"

CHAPTER 8

THE CHANGE IN PLANS

Lucy

The phone is too tight against my ear, but I can't have heard Fred properly. I step past the doorway and toward the corridor where two of my little cousins are sprawled on the floor, smacking bottle caps across the tiles with a bent spoon. Their game and laughter is loud.

"Fred?" I whisper.

"Lucy."

Just hearing the crackle as he calls my name has my legs wobbling. I grip the table edge, fingers brushing a fruit basket. The scent of ripe papayas mingles with fried onions and scorched garlic from lunch.

"Hold on." I glance around to make sure no one will be listening. Across the room, Aunt and Mama are in the kitchen, voices rising over clanging pots as they laugh about something I can't focus on. Through the glass on the veranda door, I see Alex sweeping while my little brothers dash in circles around him, yelping.

I clutch the phone tighter, walking further down the corridor, sidestepping Olivia and Juniper—nine and seven—who are deep in their crafts on the mat, snipping paper and tying string, arguing over whose scissors belong to whom.

When I make it into the back room I share with my sisters, I close the door behind me. The curtain flutters in the open window, stirring the faint scent of dust and wildflowers from the hedges outside.

"What do you mean, Safiri is in your hut?" I sink onto the bed, heart in my throat. "As your wife?"

But even as I ask, I know why. His family always wanted Safiri for Fred. A knot forms deep in my chest.

"My father." Fred's voice rasps a dull scrape against my ribs. Sounding defeated, he tells me everything—how he returned from tilling and found a curtain hanging and Safiri making herself comfortable in his house.

"Don't tell me you drank her juice." Jealousy slices through me, and I don't like it at all.

I keep my gaze locked on the colorful bracelet around my other wrist—the one he sent me with a love letter through Alex. I haven't even told him how much I love it.

"I didn't want her to get the wrong idea. I didn't. Wouldn't, Lucy."

Relief somewhat sweeps through me, but it can't brush away the angry heat. "Of course, Safiri was too willing to do as your father asked. She's been circling around your family like a fly on sugar, waiting for the right moment."

"She says she's not leaving. Thinks I'll change my mind."

I bite the inside of my cheek, hard. "I'm coming home."

"What did you say?"

Yeah, I have no idea where that came from, either. But if I don't show up, Fred might be swayed. "I want to see you."

"Aren't you supposed to be doing—what's that thing again?"

"Shadowing." I scowl at the woven mat in the corner where books are stacked. On top is the children's Bible I read to my sisters this morning. The lesson was about bravery. I'd say this situation calls for just that. "They'll have enough help without me." I still have another week off. Now, I might need to extend my break.

"Will your papa let you?"

"He and Mama are heading back to the village next week. I'll come with them."

The truck technically fits five people, but when the whole family travels together, all the kids cram into the three seats in the back, bunched up like sacks of maize.

"Lucy, I..." Fred's cautious voice rings through the speaker. The same tone he pulls up when he's trying to protect me from getting in trouble. "You already sound like you're coming before you even talk to—"

"I gotta have faith I'll see you soon."

His deep laugh reverberates through my being. "Faith. I'll cling to that until I see you."

"Well, someone has to remind Safiri she's living in a fantasy that doesn't include you." I stand and lean against Olivia and Juniper's bunk. "I'll talk to Papa properly. He needs to know it's time I take a break from shadowing anyway."

Fred exhales long and heavy. It ripples through me like a shared weight pressing between our ribs.

"But your father... How will I even see you when he's around?"

"There are goats that need pasturing." I scheme my plan. "I'll help Alex with them. Of course, now that he's saving to buy himself a solar-powered calculator, he'll be too willing to help me out."

Fred chuckles. "That boy never changes. He's always a clever businessman."

"Always dragging us into it." I laugh, warmth blooming in my chest. "Though, really, we're the ones who rope him into our plans."

"Too bad, he's the only one who can play messenger."

I grin, my heart tugging toward him like the tide. But then the thought hits—Safiri might still be in Fred's hut when I get to the village. She could be there even now.

"Where will you sleep? She's invading your space."

"John and Gertrude offered me a place to stay tonight. I'll leave early tomorrow. I need to feed the cow."

The cow I gave him. "I never asked. What did you end up naming the calf?"

"Star."

A smile spreads across my face, and my toes curl. I don't need to ask why. Stars define our memories together.

"Where will you stay tomorrow?" A whisper of fear trails my question. What if he gives in? What if they wear him down?

"If she's still there tomorrow, I'll sleep on the hill."

"The stars' hill?" My heart lifts.

"The one and only."

The hill only the two of us know. Our place to sneak off at night, counting stars until our eyes blur, heat radiating between us.

I close my eyes and imagine I'm there—right beside him. His arm curled around my shoulder, his breath warming my skin when he talks.

"I love you." The words feel like home. "No matter what."

"I love you too," he murmurs. "More than anything."

When the call ends, I just stand there, phone pressed to my chest, the stillness interrupted by the curtain rippling in the breeze. The sounds outside drift back in. A baby wailing from one of the distant rental rooms, someone yelling, perhaps scolding their child.

Then my chest aches when I picture Safiri's bare feet on Fred's floor. Her kneeling, offering him passion juice on a hot day.

I toss the phone onto my bed, consumed by one thought. How fast can I get back to the village before Fred's family decides his future?

The Bold Request

Lucy

The steamed matooke wrapped in fiber and rich peanut stew scents the dining room—real food, like home, not the bland posho we ate at school every day. The bulb above us casts a dim glow over the porcelain plates around the table. Wooden legs creak as we shift, shoulders bumping. Plates clink. Spoons scrape.

It's not as big a table as the one in the village, and the room isn't as spacious either. But here, we have light. Since Grandmother and Aunt and her family departed two hours ago and my half siblings left yesterday, this is more space than we had earlier. The Christmas holidays are winding down too soon.

On a mission, I lift a piece of dipped matooke from the sauce and pop it into my mouth, waiting for my younger siblings to stop arguing over who gets which color cup this time. They're never happy with their colors.

They're also the only ones who use plastic plates and cups so nothing breaks when they get careless.

"You two, stop!" Mama wags a finger between the boys, then resumes her conversation with Papa about the mattress they need to pick up before their departure to the village. I tap my bare feet on the cement, chewing slow, concentrating on the creamy texture coating my tongue. My mouth moves, but my mind's racing.

I've been practicing all afternoon. In front of the mirror. In my diary. I even whispered to Juniper's plastic doll when no one was in the room.

When Papa confirms the plan to Mama, he asks me to pass the salt.

I hand it to him. "Papa?" I internally breathe out.

He grunts, not looking up as he sprinkles the salt over his food.

"I was thinking..." I press my fork onto my plate, tracing a grain of rice. "When Mama and the kids go back to the village after New Year's..." Should this have been a request rather than a period? Stick to the script. "I would like to go with them. Just for a few days."

Alex kicks my shin, but I don't look at him so I can keep my serious face. It's Papa's attention I need.

He thuds the salt back on the table. Then he reaches for the rice bowl and spoons another heap onto his plate.

I peek at Mama, who side-eyes me with those knowing eyes, before I return my attention to the one person who has to grant me this request.

Papa doesn't respond. He chews, then swallows.

Maybe he didn't hear me? My lips part to ask again.

"You're staying here for a week." He reaches for his passion juice, a tightness beneath the words.

"I could use the break."

He sits up straighter, giving me that serious look—the kind that's a little rough around the edges but always shows up when he's about to drop some logic. He's an officer, for crying out loud.

"Aren't you supposed to start observing surgeries as soon as you get back?"

"I'll start observing in the second week after my return." I still have a week off, and that first week back would just be clerical work or scrubbing medical instruments. I've had enough practice in that.

"It wouldn't be wise to miss—"

"The child could use a break before she starts university." Mama sets her glass down, then leans forward. "Let her come home for a few days. It'll be a good slowdown from the city rush."

I fold my lips to hide a smile. Mama's always gentle, respectful to Papa, yet unafraid to speak up when needed. And of course, Papa, in his fierceness, always listens to her. Unless today changes that?

But there it is when his gaze meets Mama's. His shoulders relax, and the hard lines at the corners of his mouth ease. Just barely, but just enough. He holds Mama's gaze like he's reading something old and familiar in her eyes. Her smile is soft. These two sure like each other more than the many couples who marry out of necessity rather than love.

They have a moment between them like a conversation no one else at the table's meant to hear.

Then Papa breathes out a slow breath that whisks the tension out of the room like smoke.

"Fine."

"Thank you." Mama nods at Papa, who shakes his head and reaches for his drink. Probably surprised by how Mama talked him into this.

Relief flares in my chest, and I want to stand and jump and hug the two of them at the same time. But my lips press together to keep the smile from showing when Papa looks at me.

I look down at my plate. Pretending to be more interested in my food, I fork into the matooke with a trembling hand.

It's not from nerves. From hope.

"I don't want you ruining a chance at this training." Papa's gruff voice has me looking at him. "You've got a good thing at that hospital."

"I won't ruin it. I promise."

He nods once and resumes eating. The matter is done.

Mama clasps her hands together. "Well, I've been meaning to tell you more about the church I visited last week."

I didn't go last Sunday because I was called in to observe at the hospital.

Olivia perks up. "I loved how the pianist was dancing."

"The drummer said he'll teach me to play," Dennis boasts, then yelps when our littlest brother jabs him.

"*I* asked to play the drums first!"

"Isn't it wonderful?" Mama beams. "They sing and dance for Jesus like you wouldn't believe—keyboards, drums, everything. Nothing like the village church with its one sad drum."

I keep my tongue from speaking of Fred's harp. He plays it every Sunday, of course, one or two songs.

"They're having a worship night tomorrow," Mama adds. "I thought we could go."

"I can't wait," I say. Honestly, I love music, and I've never been to a church that plays piano before.

"I'm not clapping and jumping in the middle of the week." Papa waves his fork in the air. "But take the children. Church is a good enough place to keep them out of trouble."

"I wonder if the drummer will teach me how to make a drum." Alex drums his utensils on his plate, raising a clatter. "It would be good business to sell in the village someday."

"You are not making business deals in church." Mama wags a finger at him, and my laughter slips through. She has no idea what business her son is dealing with when he plays messenger. "We need to thank God for His goodness."

I glance at Alex, letting the grin escape. And now, I've even more to thank God for. I get to see Fred soon!

Mama meets my gaze as she pours juice into my cup. The knowing smile curving her lips says, "I see you. I know what you're not saying." Does she, though?

I sip the juice, the cool sweetness washing down in my throat. All I can feel is the thrum of my pulse and the countdown in my chest.

Just a few more days.

CHAPTER 9

THE MEMORIES WE MAKE

Lucy

The truck rattles along the dusty road. Each pothole jars through the suspension like we're driving over old scars. Hot, heavy air pours in through the open windows, and my soft cotton dress sticks to my back, damp with sweat. But keeping the windows shut is like getting stuck in a kitchen without windows.

My legs are numb, squashed tight between Alex and Olivia, each of us holding one of our younger siblings on our laps. Juniper keeps squirming, pressing her elbows into my ribs as she reaches for the window.

"It looks like the trees are moving!" she squeals. "The goats in the pasture—like our goats..."

She must already miss the village just like I did. I missed Fred the most.

Alex balances one of the boys—barefoot, sticky, wild-eyed—on his lap, while Olivia struggles to keep the little boy from standing every five seconds. The alternative will be sitting on top of sacks of maize, rice, and cooking oil in the open bed, jostling against bundles of clothes and baskets of fruit.

"Harrison, you don't have too much time here." Mama urges Papa to visit several locals so he can stay in tune with the community.

"I'll start with the Kabis." Papa speaks of our family friends. I'd like to see Aisha, but now that she's married, she probably doesn't have much time to wander off whenever she feels like it.

I glance out the window, my heart warming the closer we get to home, the place I once dreaded setting foot in. But, I missed the rolling hills, especially the one just out of sight—the one Fred and I slid down during that stopover in town. Cassava fields stretch toward the edge of the forest. Mango trees scatter across the land, their branches thinner than usual. The season's almost over. There aren't many mangoes left.

Dust swirls behind us, settling like mist over the dry shrubs.

We pass women returning from the well, jerricans balanced on their heads, hips swaying in rhythm with the road. Some pause to wave. Others just stare like they're studying a storm cloud that might pass or pour. The children beam as they wave, each with a smaller jerrican on their heads. My younger siblings peer out the window, asking Papa to stop and give the village kids a ride in the truck.

"Even if we want to, where would everyone sit?" Papa asks.

Mama twists in the front seat to smile at us. "Maybe on one of Papa's visits to church, he can bring the truck and give the kids a ride."

The truck isn't new. But it's still a spectacle here where bicycles rule the road and we are the only ones with a car.

Soon, we're rounding the bend to our expansive property, passing the cow stalls surrounded by overgrown trees and shrubs. A cow moos, and I grin.

The house's familiar outline appears behind a broad deciduous tree just as I remember it—stucco walls, Spanish tile roof, and the brick kitchen off to the side, smoke curling from its chimney. The compound is alive—chickens darting about, the goat house visible in the distance. It all warms me.

Edna and Seza rush out to greet us.

"I missed you." I wrap one of our housekeepers in a hug. I'm fond of both, but I click with Edna the most.

It takes over an hour to unload. A new mattress for the guest room. Baskets of apples and the kind of papayas we don't grow here. New cooking pots, jerricans of oil, sacks of flour and sugar, and bunches of matooke since Busobi soil doesn't favor this type of banana.

Much later, after we've settled, Papa swaps his collared shirt for an old threadbare button-down, faded at the elbows and missing the top button, trying to pass as one of the locals. He looks less like a government worker now, more like a village elder.

"I'm going to catch up with the neighbors." He straddles his dusty bicycle.

"Don't be late for supper." Mama waves him off from the doorway where she stands.

When he leaves, she announces she's taking a nap and urges us to do the same.

"I'll help Edna with supper," I say, plotting a way to reconnect with Fred. Now, where did Alex vanish off to?

"We're going to use our new rockets!" The boys dart to their room.

Olivia takes Juniper's hand. "We've been eager to make table mats with palm leaves."

I head for the kitchen building, the scent of woodsmoke and roasted peanuts wrapping around me like a memory.

Edna sits in the round twig chair near the firepit, peeling matooke. Her frame is sturdy, her soft lines etched deep in concentration.

"Oh, Edna." I pull a stool closer to her. "I missed you so much."

She lifts her head, eyes warm. Her chuckles rumbles low and knowing. "I can tell. That smile says a lot."

Years of smoke have darkened the kitchen walls, but the rhythm of the place feels like home, even though I've rarely been here in the village. I slide a loose log further into the firepit, the dry bark scratching my arm.

Everything here brings me back—the nights I snuck in to heat milk for Cutie, the goat house Fred cleaned in my stead. Or the time he showed up drenched from the rain, just to talk, both of us shoulder to shoulder by the fire.

"Are the villagers embracing Mama yet?" I sink to sit on the floor.

"Most will always be driven by jealousy." Edna flips a peeled banana before tossing it into the pan with the others. "They're coming around, though. No one turns down food when she hosts the women's sewing events. But your aunt still makes noise. Thinks she can control your mama."

We fall into easy chatter as she recounts the latest village gossip—the usual tiffs and the never-ending feud between Fred's father and my aunt.

"Not sure they'll ever get along," she mutters. "I think they still like each other deep down. But what's left between them is just anger and noise."

My chest twinges with a pang of sympathy. If they still care, that's even sadder. "They're both married now."

"Even if one of Fred's father's wives dies, he still has two more. So it's not like he'd ever be single again."

"Nobody's dying." I hope nothing bad happens to any of them. "My aunt is married too. Everyone's moved on."

I shift the conversation to happier things, sharing my time in the city and shadowing at the hospital. "It's been fine there, but... I wish I was here. For the holidays. With you."

Edna lifts an eyebrow. "You mean with Fred."

Heat floods my neck. I glance toward the doorway, making sure no one else is around to hear. Leaning in, I whisper, "He's the main reason I came back."

He'll come tonight. Unless Gertrude never relayed the message about my arrival date.

Once Edna finishes peeling, I take the banana peels to the goat house. The wide compound makes me want to run through it, there is so much possibility to this expansive space. The late afternoon sun spills golden light over the dirt, and chickens scratch and peck near the shrubs. I shift the basket in my arms.

Then a rock skips across the ground.

A chicken shrieks and launches into the air in a flurry of feathers.

I'd be sprinting off in panic if it wasn't still daytime. Still, my heart hammers as I spin toward the thick green shrubs where the rock originated.

Oh my! Fred. Peeking from behind the avocado tree. His hair could use a trim. It shadows eyes twinkling with mischief. My breath catches. The basket drops from my arms and thuds into the dust, peels scattering.

His smile is brighter than the sun, and my heart is melting. He raises his hand and waves.

My feet lift off the ground, and I break into a sprint. My sandals slap the packed earth, then crunch against dry twigs. I dash into the shrubbery, ducking behind the tree where he waits.

"Fred!"

He steps out fully, arms open wide, and I crash into him. His arms wrap around me, strong and steady. My face presses into his chest, the scent of soap and sun and Fred engulfing me.

"Lucy." He breathes my name, laughing, and I laugh too. We're both breathless, relieved like we've waited longer than we admit.

"I thought you'd never get here." His breath warms my cheek. Then his lips press to my temple. "I've been hiding behind that tree for four hours."

I pull back enough to take him in. He's wearing the Sunday shirt I bought him last year. The one he only wears on special days.

"I can tell you didn't do farmwork today."

"I fed the cows this morning. That counts."

I mock glare. "You threw a rock at me."

"To scare the chicken." He ducks his head, sheepish. "It worked."

Sinking into his shoulder, I let my body relax. "I missed you so much."

He pulls back and brushes tangled strands from my face. His fingertips linger. "Let me see you. You look..."

"Tired? Sweaty?" Of course, I showered and changed into a flowery pink dress. "Like I've been squished in a truck for five hours?"

"Beautiful," he finishes without flinching.

I bite my lip, heart aching and glowing all at once. "You're not supposed to say things like that in public. What if someone sees?"

He leans in, mouth close to my ear. "Birds and bugs don't gossip."

Just then, someone calls out. "Lucy!"

Ugh. Alex.

I roll my eyes and grab Fred's hand, tugging him farther behind the tree. He's already a step ahead. His lips crash onto mine, an arm curling around my waist as my hand rises to his cheek. His stubble pricks my fingers, and we kiss with urgency and desperation until we're breathless.

"Tonight?" I whisper.

"I was counting on stargazing."

"Meet at the creek?" Our meeting place.

He winks. "I'll have the ladder at your window for you."

So thoughtful of him. My lips curl up. "Don't get caught."

"I won't."

I start to move.

But he tugs me back, his expression shifting. "Safiri's still at the house."

The words crush my chest. Each one sears like hot sauce squeezed into a wound.

"I haven't been staying there." His eyes, loaded with a tenderness and love that eases the stiffness in my shoulders, search mine. "I made a temporary shelter near our hill. I only go back to take food at home and feed the cows."

How does he cook? Drink clean water if it's not boiled? My lips part to ask. But we have tonight. I nod and press my hand to his chest. A thrumming pulses beneath my fingertips. "Tell me everything. Tonight."

"Tonight," he repeats. Then, swallowing, he takes my hand from his heart and kisses my palm. Tingles shoot up my arm. Wow, Fred has grown a lot in this kissing department.

Supper drags. The matooke, peanut sauce, and meat taste flat in my mouth as my mind races. I'm already under the stars, Fred beside me, as we trace constellations with his fingers.

When we all retreat to our rooms, I lie still as my sisters' breaths go heavy.

Finally, I climb out the window like I'm not an adult. But that's the thing about being eighteen—you're old enough to know what you want, but still answering to the people who pay your school fees. Papa won't approve of me seeing Fred. So that keeps me sneaking around.

The Dreamers' Hill

Lucy

Stars blink like they've been waiting for an audience, waiting for us. They hang low and bright, scattered across the dark sky. Crickets chirp as Fred's battery-operated torch brightens our path. His other hand clasps mine, warm and comforting, like he won't let go. We walk uphill in companionable silence where every breath is familiar, every step a memory retraced.

He flashes a light on his makeshift house.

I nudge him. "Impressive." He's built it with logs and wrapped a tarp around it. But... "What if snakes go inside?"

"I have metal roofing as the door. I'll show you in the daylight if we get time during your visit."

When we reach the hill, he urges me to climb first, holding up the flashlight so I can see the steps he dug into the slope.

My backpack is light—just a blanket and the sweets I brought for him. At the top, I flash the light down for him.

"I've been here so many times"—he waves the light away—"I could climb it with my eyes closed."

Before I can unzip the bag, he's already beside me.

"I brought us a blanket." He flashes the light toward a worn brown one already spread over the grass. Threads dangle loose at the corners. He settles down and pats the space beside him. "It's not fancy. But I'm glad I kept an extra. Used it when I was in school."

"I love it." I fold my legs under me, the cotton soft beneath them. "Because it's yours." Not Safiri's. I lower my backpack and pull out the goodies I brought. "Biscuits." I hand him the tin, then a wrapped parcel. "I hope you like this."

His fingers tremble as he unwraps the cloth slowly, like it's swaddling something fragile. The torch rests beside him now, its glow soft.

"A pen... and a book." Wonder fills his voice, the same wonder I felt when I learned he wished to go back to school someday. Now, he has.

"A diary," I clarify. "From the hospital gift shop. And the pen doesn't smudge. In case you ever get around to writing those poems you said helped you pass your English exam."

I try to keep my voice light, but my heart trips. If only I could track down the examiners who grade the national exams and read the essays he wrote about me.

He turns the journal over in his hands, fingers tracing the spine as if it were pure gold. I didn't expect him to look at it like it meant more than I knew how to say. "I'll use it," he promises. "But only when I'm writing about you."

I roll my eyes. "You're getting smooth about romance. You know that?"

He leans in, breath warm against my ear. "Learned from the best."

His lips graze just beneath it, and I shiver, goose bumps breaking out along my arms despite the warm night.

We lie back against the slope, shoulder to shoulder, eyes tilted toward the heavens. The dry grass beneath us crunches and pokes through the thin blanket, but I ignore the discomfort.

Fred either doesn't notice or doesn't care. If he's uncomfortable, it's the least of his worries.

"Starting next week..." I'm not sure where to begin with all we have to talk about. "They'll let me observe inside the wards, not just filing paperwork. Real patients."

"That's wonderful. I'm proud of you." His hand finds mine, his fingers warm and steady. "Even if I don't like being far from you, I'm happy for you, Lucy."

I squeeze his hand back. "My days here are few. Let's make the most of the time we have."

He turns to look at me, his eyes catching the starlight like water. "I don't want this night to end."

And I don't either. "Luckily, it's only just started."

I lean forward, and our lips meet in a kiss that makes the world blur and hush. The dry grass crackles beneath us, the sky stretching wide above, heavy with stars. All I feel is his breath, the press of his mouth, and the thrum of something deeper anchoring us to this moment—just us, nothing else.

When we pull apart, our breaths come uneven and close.

"If tomorrow works out"—he pauses, gulping in breath—"I want to take you back."

"Back... where?"

"The field of dahlias."

My breath catches. My voice barely rises above a whisper. "You remember that?"

"Of course. I remember every single moment with you." His thumb traces along my jaw with tenderness. "You turned eighteen that day. You were wearing striped shorts and a green blouse. Your smile... You laughed so hard when I drove you in the wheelbarrow. Distracted by your presence, I almost tipped us into a tree, but you were having too much fun to notice. The picnic, the songs..."

I smile into the starry night, the memory so vivid it flickers like a scene playing in the sky above us. "I brought more batteries. Want me to bring the radio?"

"I still have the ones you gave me. The big red one, the pocket size one with the cracked knob, and the silver. I've added more songs to our list."

My cheeks ache from smiling, and something deeper presses against my ribs. Tears threaten when my throat tightens. He found a field of my favorite flowers for our picnic last year. And he remembers the day so vividly. Does he really remember every moment we've shared?

"Fred?" I shift my hand to his chest, his cotton T-shirt soft between my fingers. "That was one of the best days of my life."

"We'll celebrate your birthday early this year." His fingertips, rough from work, trace a circle on my cheek, and I suck in a breath. He remembers my birthday too. It's after I return to the city. "Let's make this one outdo the last."

CHAPTER 10

THE FIELD OF DREAMS

Fred

The morning breeze stirs the trees, gentle, unlike my racing heart. Goats bleat somewhere. And I pace near the path where Lucy should appear any minute now. Years of hooves have carved the footpath to the grazing field, mostly from the officer's animals since they're the only ones in the village with a real herd.

I've been up since dawn, unable to sit still.

This day must be perfect.

My hands are damp from gripping the dahlias I picked and tied with banana fiber. It's too simple for what I want this to mean.

But it's what I have.

A whistle snaps my attention toward the path, and my heart claps like thunder when they approach.

Only Lucy makes my chest soar like this. Only she could make me eager for a day blistered with heat.

Her laugh rises as she talks to her brother, the sound like rain drenching dry land. She's woven her hair into two braids, and they bounce against her shoulder with each step. The long, staff-like stick in her hand moves as she talks. And even from here, her playful energy revives me.

Alex sees me first. He squints into the sunlight, then elbows her, and points.

Lucy tosses the stick, and my feet lift off the crumpled grass. I'm striding across the uneven field. But when I reach her, the bundle of dahlias feels ridiculous.

And yet, the smile she gives me—bright and effortless—tells me she doesn't care whether I come with something or nothing.

I stop short of pulling her into my arms. Instead, I hold out the flowers—too fast, too hard. A few petals break loose and float between us like pieces of breath.

"These are for you." How can I even speak with how hard I'm breathing? I might as well have run a marathon.

She blinks, then reaches for the bouquet. Her fingers graze mine. "They're beautiful."

Then she closes the space between us. She barely has her arms around me when mine circle her waist, pulling her closer.

The silk of her blue outfit—a one-piece with shorts—is soft beneath my hands. Her hair smells like something bright and clean, a perfume I can't name, but it heals something raw in me—the something hollowed out by weeks of missing her.

Alex clears his throat. Only then, do I remember we're not alone.

I loosen my arms, and we both glance at her brother.

"I'll just... take the goats and leave you two." He waves vaguely toward the stretch of grass where the animals have wandered. "Four hours. I'll be back then."

"Thanks, brother." She winks.

I nod, grateful for the four hours—better than the two we had last time.

I step out of the embrace and take her free hand in mine.

Alex's voice follows us as he turns away. "You two better not do anything foolish."

"Alex! Leave!" Lucy calls back, laughing.

He shoots me a warning glare like I'm not three years older than he is.

"I'll behave." I call back loud enough for him to hear. I know what he means. Even with the ache I carry for her—how often she fills my thoughts, my dreams—I wouldn't ruin what we have. Not for anything.

So I lead her to a narrow path winding through the shrubs. "I thought today we'd walk." A shrub scrapes against my elbow. "No wheelbarrow."

She grins, then tugs me ahead, the hem of her loose shorts swaying. "Then I get to memorize every detail of this place."

I catch up to her pace. Dahlias in orange, white, red, and yellow decorate the path like scattered confetti.

"I don't remember this many dahlias last time." She brushes her bouquet over the tips as we pass into the full field.

"I made a few improvements."

She spins to face me. "Don't tell me you planted more dahlias?"

At my nod, her hand drops from mine. She presses her fingers to her lips and gasps. "How?"

"The seeds that fell off... I figured I'd sprinkle them around." I'm glad she came back when they were in full bloom.

Her head tilts. Her eyes glisten. "Oh, Fred."

My chest puffs out, blooming with excitement. How am I supposed to handle the way she's looking at me—like I've handed her the stars?

So I motion toward the umbrella tree. "We'd better get to the food before the monkeys do."

She laughs, and we start walking again. The monkeys prefer bananas, but if they're desperate, even papayas don't stand a chance.

Under the deciduous tree, we settle on the blanket spread over the woven mat. Faint rays of sunlight dapple the shade on the opposite side. I'll move the mat once the sun shifts.

From the covered basket, I retrieve cassava chips, banana chips, and the two orange sodas I bought in town.

"Such special treatment." Lucy lifts the bottle to her mouth. "But I want you to drink that one."

"I bought all these for you."

She hands me her open soda. "How about we share?"

When she winks, I take it, our hands brushing. I try to ignore the sparks shooting up my arm yet again from any contact.

"Sorry the soda isn't cold." The drink is hot compared to the cold one we shared in town.

"You did all this?" Folding her legs beneath her, she gestures toward the now-wilted bouquets wrapped at each corner of the mat. "It's perfect."

My heart squeezes as I look at her rounded lips, her flawless face. How is it that she's here with me? That she loves me despite our different backgrounds? "You... are perfect."

We take turns sipping sodas and eating chips. She lets out delightful appreciation when she bites into some papaya. "I've missed papayas."

"I'll be sure you eat plenty of them while you're around."

"How is it"—her voice dips quieter—"with Safiri still at your house?"

Of course, she'd ask. It's embarrassing having no control over the situation while my father runs my life.

Birds flock from the tree and into the shrubs. Like me, fleeing my roost. "I barely see her. I stop in for clothes and to check on Mama and the cow and calf. I keep my things locked in my suitcase."

She watches me closely. "And she doesn't try... to talk to you?"

"I don't give her the chance."

Lucy's hand rubs my shoulder, and I look at her. She must catch my sincerity because she nods. "Okay."

I let out my held breath when she rolls onto her stomach, dropping the subject. I do the same, and we lie side by side, arms brushing.

She nudges me. "Play the songs you promised you added to the playlist."

I already have a disc in the radio. One push of a button and a song filters through—the kind that always makes my chest ache—"Every Time You Go Away."

She hums along, then leans into me. "This isn't new."

She gave me the CD last year.

"It's our song." I brush my thumb in slow circles over her wrist, and she shivers. "It plays in my head when I miss you most."

"It plays in mine too."

The warmth between us spreads—low and electric. The melody floats through the still air, a ballad of distance and longing, like someone missing air and remembering how to breathe.

When the song fades, her lips graze my cheek. "And now I'm here."

A slow, full feeling blooms in my chest. With her beside me, everything else fades—no problems, no future worries. Just this.

I kiss her cheek, soft and lingering. "Wherever you are makes the scenery perfect."

"The feeling's mutual." She nudges me playfully. "Now, let's hear your supposed new list. I want proof."

I switch the CD, and the upbeat melody reminds me of her energy. It's a song about sketching out tomorrows and the kind of love that survives storms.

She loops her arm through mine. "You made this CD?"

"With John's help."

Another song plays—"Ghost"—and my heart tightens, the lyrics drawing out all the weeks I went without her.

She sniffles, clearly moved. "Fred..." Her voice cracks. "That's the sweetest song."

"I didn't mean to make you cry." I thumb the tear from her cheek.

We stay like that, quiet, until the music fades into stillness.

Then she shifts and selects a slice of papaya. She pokes it with the sharpened stick resting in the bowl. "UCE results come out soon." Her words match her movements, slow, thoughtful. "Less than a month."

"UNEB for both of us," I say. "Then everything shifts."

She nods. "Are you nervous?"

I could lie. Pretend to be fine, but this is Lucy, not my father, whom I have to prove I'm a strong man. "I'm terrified. What if I fail and don't get sponsorship?"

"You're going to get sponsorship." She edges closer. "If I hadn't switched to sciences, maybe we would've ended up at the same university? Makerere, perhaps."

"Do you know how expensive Makerere is?" How could she think I could get into that university? "I'm sure it's even harder to get sponsorships there. All that competition."

"You're very smart, Fred."

Her confidence in me sends my heart pounding with fear. What if I don't make it? If I fail, I'll be letting her down too.

Done with this conversation, I switch the topic. "Are you excited to start observing surgeries?"

"I can't wait." Her face lights up as she talks about the unknown, ready to conquer anything thrown at her. The conversation flows like it always has, easy and natural, but beneath it all, lingers a pull of questions we don't know the answers to.

We talk, we laugh, and we let time slip away. It always vanishes faster than I'd like. I don't even notice until a sharp whistle zings out in the distance.

"I forgot my watch." Lucy rubs her bare wrist.

"We better not keep Alex waiting if we want his help again." I rise and offer my hand. She takes it without hesitation.

I'll come back later to gather my things. Right now, all that matters is walking her back.

Just before we reach the clearing where we can see Alex waiting through the shrubs, I stop. I pull her into me, one hand on her waist, the other cupping her cheek. Our lips meet in a kiss that says what words can't— *"Stay. Don't go. Come back soon."*

Her mouth is warm, familiar. And for a moment, the world holds still again.

When we part, her breath catches. I lean my forehead to hers.

"Do you want to meet at the water pump tomorrow?" she asks.

I raise a brow. The pump is gossip central for the village women. "People will talk."

She grins, eyes glinting. "Let them."

I cup her face again, not ready to let go. "I'll be lurking in the bushes as soon as I can."

"We won't be that early." She slaps my chest, her laugh playful.

"I'm not taking any chances." I smile. "I'll come after I finish a few things at home."

At home.

Everything is different there.

Come morning, I endure a different kind of pain as if yesterday I wasn't floating on clouds in Lucy's presence. If I could avoid this breakfast at Mama's house, I would, but I don't want to hurt Mama. She works so hard to make sure I'm fed before I go cultivating the fields.

I duck as I enter her hut, and porridge fills my senses. "You're just in time, my dear." Mama carries a plate of leftover sweet potatoes to the table. I do my best to ignore Safiri as my siblings swam me for a greeting.

Finally, I sit, and my gaze lands where it shouldn't. On the mat where Safiri sits. Her hair is short but nicely combed back, her eyes soft as they meet mine.

I refocus on Mama.

She returns to the makeshift table. Steam rises as she spoons porridge into mugs. "We're almost out of the sugar you got us, so this will be the last porridge with sugar." Her tone is too bright, like it's meant to drown out the tension that sits between us like smoke.

"Good morning, Fred," Safiri says finally.

I nod, avoiding eye contact.

"I made some chapati last night, but you didn't come home for supper."

I keep my gaze on the leftovers. Father usually sits in the empty chair on the other side. I'm just glad he's not here this morning.

Next thing I know, she's kneeling and putting a plate of chapati beside me.

"Thank you." I hand it over to Viola. "You can split this with everyone."

"Fred?" Mama hisses as she places porridge on the table. "Your wife made you chapati."

"She's not my wife." I speak through gritted teeth, snatch the mug from Mama, and lift it to my mouth. I sputter as the metal cup burns my lips.

I'm not cruel. But I can't give Safiri or anyone hope I don't carry. I stand, take the potato in my hand. "Thanks for breakfast, Mama." I nod toward the door. "Got to go feed the cows."

Mama glances at her untouched food on the mat, then at Safiri seated not far from her. My siblings are busy fighting over who Viola gave the bigger portion of chapati. "We haven't started eating yet."

"I'll leave you to it." Yes, this is the third time Safiri has joined in for breakfast. I don't like it one bit. Not that my parents respect my wishes.

I step outside, and Mama's voice bounces off my back. I ignore her and march across the compound. "Fred," she calls again.

I turn to see her emerge, then wait as her bare feet hit the dusty ground.

"You can't keep treating her this way," she says, voice low, tight. "Your father arranged—"

"I didn't ask for this arrangement." Fury burns in my chest. "I've been respectful."

"Respectful? You walk past her like she's invisible." Mama's arms cross her chest. "That girl came back with the officer, didn't she?"

In Viola's excitement to see Lucy, which I haven't arranged yet, she might have slipped, and now Mama knows Lucy is in town. Either way. "Lucy's not 'that girl.' She's—"

"She's from a family that walks like they're better than the rest of us," Mama snaps. "Her mother looks down her nose at everyone just because her husband is no farmer."

"Primrose is not like that." My voice rises over the children crying inside. "Lucy is not some girl."

"No?"

What else can I say to earn my parents' support on this? Because I could tell her Lucy's the most grounded person I know. That she takes care of her siblings. That she listens to me when no one else does.

They already act like Safiri and I are married. Oh, come to think of it, we don't even need to have an official ceremony to be considered married. The longer she stays in my house, the more I need to build a different house somewhere else, away from this compound.

"I need to go." The sweet potato stains my hands now. I have no appetite.

I won't give up on Lucy. Not for tradition. Not even for my mother. I just need to enjoy the few days—mere hours in the day—I have left with Lucy.

CHAPTER 11

THE UNEXPECTED MOMENTS

Fred

I bring Viola along to meet Lucy at the pump. I convince Mama to let her help me with the planting. She'll drop maize seeds while I dig the holes. The real task will happen way after Lucy leaves.

The moment Viola spots Lucy, she lets out a shriek and flings her arms around her, hugging her tight. Watching them, I can't help but wonder if I welcomed my girlfriend the right way. We're not a hugging kind of family. But being around Lucy changes that—changes a lot of things Viola and I never grew up doing.

While Lucy's siblings and housekeepers line up for water meters away, I linger by the sugarcane, close enough to hear Viola and Lucy catching up—talking fabrics, patterns, and sewing new designs someday.

"Now that I won't be running a boutique." Lucy's voice is softer. "I hope you can carry that dream for me... until you find your own path."

"I would love that!" Viola bounces on her toes, glowing. "Can you take me to the city someday?"

"You can count on it." Lucy pulls her into another hug.

My smile stretches wide. Something about Lucy brings out a different spark in Viola—a light I don't see often.

I tune out the whispers that trail us from women balancing water on their heads, babies strapped to their backs. Let them talk.

I wanted this time alone with Lucy, but it's Viola's only chance to see her. With the jerricans filled, we walk side by side with Lucy and her family—me hauling Lucy's jerrican in one hand and her sister's in the other. No sign of Alex at the well. He's probably stuck with heavier chores back at the house.

"I hope you're not planning to follow us all the way." Edna stops as we reach the creek that cuts across their land.

"I'll leave you here." I set the water down, and Viola darts forward to hug Lucy again.

"I'll see you sooner than later." Lucy hugs her back just as fiercely.

Her sister nudges a smaller jerrican toward me. "Can you lift it to my head?"

When I do, she follows Edna across the rocks leading into the creek.

Then Lucy leans close and murmurs. "Tonight. At the hill?"

I nod, heart thudding. Anticipation thrums beneath my skin, and I battle the urge to kiss her, aware Edna could turn around any second.

But Lucy doesn't hesitate. Her lips brush mine—warm, certain, and full of promises that send my pulse into a sprint. "I'll see you tonight."

"Tonight." My voice is hoarse, and my hands tremble. Everything in me begs me to kiss her again. But that can wait until... "Tonight."

The Land We Build On

Fred

The rest of the week blurs into stolen moments, each one slipping through my fingers too fast. Lucy spends more time with me than with her family, but our time together still feels too short.

On her last evening, I can't wait for nightfall. I hide behind the kitchen, hoping she might wander this way. Truth is, I'm always hoping to run into her, even in the empty fields she never walks through.

The kitchen staff trickles off toward the coop, one by one. Footsteps crunch on gravel. Voices carry. I press flat against the brick wall, heart thudding.

Alex rounds the corner. His eyes widen when he sees me, but before he can say anything, Primrose appears behind him. At least it's not the officer.

"Good evening... um, madam."

"What a surprise to see you here." Primrose smiles, her kind eyes full of unspoken questions.

"Oh, Fred," Alex jumps in, tone easy. "I completely forgot to bring those books for your sister."

I blink, then nod, catching on. "Yeah. Viola couldn't wait till tomorrow. Thanks for letting her borrow them."

Primrose's soft brown eyes search mine. She's not buying the book excuse, is she?

"Why didn't you just come to the house?"

"Uh, the officer is—"

"I know you two had a bump. But that was last year." Her smile widens, and before I can recover, she adds, "Why don't you stay for supper?"

I nearly choke. The officer won't welcome me with open arms, but if I can catch even two seconds with Lucy before getting booted out, I'll risk it. Still, I try to play it cool. "I wouldn't want to impose."

"Nonsense." She waves in the kind of gesture that leaves no room for argument. I don't push it, not when it works in my favor.

Just like that, I find myself at their table, trying not to stare as Lucy leans over to ladle beef stew onto the bed of rice on my plate. With her father's gaze pinned on me, I'm terrified to look at him long enough to catch his expression.

"Lucy says you've been in school," he says once Lucy finishes filling my plate.

"Yes, sir." I clear my voice. One wrong word, and he'll send me out of his house before the meal ends. "I sat for both my ordinary and advanced level exams. Just waiting on the results now."

His brows lift. "How'd you manage to take both in one year?" With that clipped tone, he's testing me, assuming I'm lying. "For someone who hadn't been in school at all, that's a big leap."

"The headmaster in town helped." I rub my clumsy hands together on my lap and peek at Lucy. Her eyes are wide. She's probably afraid I'll mention her efforts in this. I'm not that stupid. "I'm grateful," I add, still looking at her, even though my answer is for her father.

"What are your plans once the results come in?"

"If I pass and can get a sponsorship, I'd like to study literature and education. I want to teach."

His nod is slow, meditative. "Not many young men have clear intentions."

"Fred's always been different." Pride threads through Lucy's voice.

The officer glances at her, then back at me. "Different can be good, but you know how hard it is to get a sponsorship. Your scores have to be among the top five percent in the entire country to even have a chance."

My stomach twists. I knew it wouldn't be easy, but hearing it bluntly slams like a brick into my chest.

"I hope you've saved some money," he adds, his gaze steady, "in case you don't get funded."

I reach for my spoon and scoop some rice, forcing myself to eat, but my appetite is gone.

"I know God has a plan, sweetheart." Primrose's gentle voice carries through the air. "I'm sure it wasn't easy for your father to support you, but we're proud of you for taking that step of faith into the unknown."

I swallow, then nod. "Thank you." But my father isn't proud of me. Not even close.

"Did you know Harrison is the only one in his family who went to school?" Primrose sets her fork down.

"Really?" I feign surprise, even though Lucy told me that about her father.

Primrose touches her husband's arm. When he glances her way, she lifts a brow. A quiet tenderness passes between them.

The officer meets my gaze. "Farming wasn't the only path." He doesn't offer more. "I wish you the best."

It isn't much. But coming from him, it feels like a blessing. And that means more than I expected.

As I prepare to leave, I nod my farewell to Lucy. Her smile melts something in my chest, the way it always does.

She lifts a hand in a gentle wave. "It was nice to see you, Fred. I hope I'll be back in the village someday."

My heart pounds. I ignore the ache twisting inside me. My lips part, and my gaze holds hers. The silent pain is too much to bear, but the kick to my shin under the table is Alex's warning that

I'm about to get caught if I don't stop looking at Lucy like this. "Goodbye. Lucy." I don't look at her again. To Alex and their siblings, I offer a quick, "See you soon, maybe at church."

"Come back when you get some time," Primrose calls. "I always have work for you to do."

"Thank you, madam."

I glance toward the officer, expecting silence. But he rises, tips his head toward the door, and walks me out. Not Lucy. Him. He must have caught me staring at his daughter.

At the threshold, his tall frame blocks the doorway, and I suck in a breath, braced for a reprimand.

"I was harsh last year. Maybe too harsh."

What? Is that... an apology? No man around here ever admits fault—especially not to a woman or someone younger.

Hope flares in my chest. I square my shoulders, arms at my sides, grounding myself. "Thank you... for supper, sir."

"Take care of yourself, Fred."

Who is this man? And what happened to the fierce officer this whole village fears—myself included? Maybe Primrose's kindness softens his edges. Maybe it's something else. Either way, God must be on my side tonight.

Lucy and I didn't get a proper goodbye, but now, I can stop by if she's ever back in the village. Whether her father's home or not. Next time, I won't have to sneak around.

Swept up in happiness, I stay the night on the hill, half hoping Lucy might escape and show up. But again, I'm not sure how, but

I hope I'll see her soon. Maybe I'll go to the city to visit her. I can stay in a hotel now that I have some money.

That would mean forgetting to save for school, though.

After dawn, I trudge back to our compound to feed the cows. Dew sticks to my hands and the exposed parts of my feet not shielded by my rubber sandals.

The compound is eerily quiet, but the roosters crow. I smile, wondering if Lucy has already left by now.

I pause at my hut, where the curtain sways. My stomach churns. Safiri kept me *from my own house*. My previous happiness vanishes.

Then she steps out and dumps water into the dirt. She looks at me coldly. She's wearing a brown dress that falls to her ankles. She then goes back inside.

I walk toward Mama's side of the compound, where the cow and her calf stay in trees.

Father steps out of Mama's hut. Seems they worked things out if he stayed the night there.

So much for my good mood. My heart sinks. "Good morning, Father."

"Fred." His voice booms. His blue button-down is worn, but he's dressed like he's on a mission. His jaw clenches. "Safiri is packing to leave."

"Good." I shrug. Why should that be a concern of mine?

"If you won't stay with your wife—"

"She's not my wife."

"She's in your house now. You can stop her from leaving." He jams his fists to his hips. "She could be your wife traditionally. But since you've rejected her... you won't stay here at all."

I stare at him. "What?"

"No being on this land."

I blink, stunned. "I built my house."

"On my land."

The words slam into me like a wall. For a moment, the only sound is the distant cluck of chickens and the wind pushing dust across the yard.

CHAPTER 12

The Shadow

Lucy

The operating theater is colder than I expected. Goose bumps prickle my arms beneath the oversized scrubs as I stand against the wall, trying to blend into the tiles. Six observers crowd the space, four interns and two of us just observing and holding our breath.

"Scalpel." Dr. Namuganza's voice remains calm despite the tension in the room. A nurse places it in her gloved hand.

The first incision is clean. A thin line of red appears across the patient's abdomen, and I force myself not to look away. This is what I came for. This is what I want.

"What we're looking at," Dr. Namuganza explains without looking up, "is a bowel obstruction. Common enough, but deadly if left untreated. Notice the distention here."

She gestures with her instrument, and we all crane forward.

"Sometimes, these resolve on their own. Often, they don't. The key is recognizing the signs early—persistent pain, vomiting, absence of bowel movements or gas. In rural areas especially, patients arrive too late."

Rural areas. Like home. If I ever worked in the village. But no way. I like the convenience of the city too much.

Besides the medical terms, I enjoy watching the procedures. Even now, as the doctor moves her hands steadily, I can tell she's had years of training.

"This procedure doesn't always require surgery. Sometimes, decompression methods work—nasogastric tubes, rectal tubes for lower obstructions. But you need to know when those won't be enough."

Excited by learning something like this, I take it all in. Later, I'll delve further into this topic in my textbooks.

February arrives with scattered rains—and hope. The first set of national exam results is out.

It's evening. The hospital corridors have quieted to a low hum of machines and murmured conversation. I'm in the storage room, pulling out boxes of gloves and unpacking new patient gowns when my phone buzzes against my hip.

Gertrude's name flashes on the screen.

"Fred?" My joy emerges in a rush of giddy breath.

"UCE results are back." As he speaks, I picture the grin in his words. "I passed, Lucy. All subjects. Flying colors."

I press the phone tighter to my ear, eyes squeezed shut. He's worked so hard, even lost his home now. I still ache thinking of him camping out, off his father's land. But now isn't the time for sad thoughts. "I knew you would! Tell me everything!"

His laugh bursts through warm, and unguarded. In my mind, we're in an open field, jumping, screaming, laughing like kids who just touched the sky.

"Religious education, I got a B, but that only shows I need to read the Bible more."

"I'm so proud of you." My legs wobble, so I lean against the shelves of gauze and antiseptic. "So, so proud."

"Have you been able to watch any more surgeries without fainting?"

"That was only one time."

I tell him about the procedures I've witnessed—appendectomies, C-sections, the bowel obstruction from earlier this week. He listens intently as I describe each one, and his questions prove how much he's absorbed from our conversations about medicine.

"You're going to be an amazing doctor."

His sincerity makes my chest ache. "And you're going to be an amazing teacher. Or writer in case you go that route too."

"I'd better stick to teaching if the village is going to be any different."

"You'll do wonderful." But while I love the thought of him teaching in the village, I can't shake the fear that village life isn't meant for me when we reach the point of finished careers and settled lives.

Someone calls my name beyond the door. It's probably one of the nurses on night rounds. I volunteered to stay an extra three hours since they were three observers short today.

"I have to go," I admit, despite my reluctance to end our happy celebration. "Night rounds are starting. But, Fred, I'm so proud of you. This is just the beginning."

"Just the beginning," he repeats, and excitement for our future lifts me, like I'm weightless, floating somewhere above the clouds.

February bleeds into March like watercolors on wet paper if heavy rainfall and muddy dirt roads are any indication. This time of year, the muddy barracks are not my favorite place. It's worse because Molly and Hugh went back to their village to be with their mother before school starts. Spending time at the hospital has been a good distraction.

I stay connected to Molly, Hugh and Fred through hurried phone calls. My hands are clammy with water as I fold the umbrella before the hospital veranda. I glimpse a newspaper stand with bold headlines—UACE Results Released!

My pulse starts racing. Not for me. For Fred.

As soon as I get into the storage area where we keep our bags, I call Gertrude's shop.

"Lucy." Her typical cheerful greeting warms me.

I ask as usual about her and how business is going before asking if Fred knows the results arrived yet.

"No, dear. But John told him to come back this week to see if the results are in."

"I'm sure he'll call me as soon as he gets his results."

"Your young man will be fine, Lucy." She must sense my concern. "He's a smart one."

"Thank you, Gertrude."

"Have you seen your results yet?"

"I just found out. I'm sure Papa will drop everything to fetch them from school before the day ends."

With a promise to talk soon, I hang up.

The Results

Lucy

Four days. Four long days of anticipating and waiting to hear from Fred. He probably still has no idea the exams are back. But if John told him to return to town this week, why would he wait so long?

I bite into the chapati rolled in with eggs and fixate on the birds hovering around the courtyard for crumbs we can throw their way. My results have been back for eternity. By the time I got off work the day I saw the paper, Papa had already returned with the certificate.

My results are good enough to get me into the top nursing school—exactly the one Papa had been eyeing for me, affiliated with one of the biggest hospitals in the country. I didn't qualify for a sponsorship, but Papa wasn't counting on that and already set money aside.

"Next week, I'll go ahead and pay the deposit." He told me over supper as we reviewed my transcript. "Housing's competitive. If you pay early, you get priority for campus dorms."

The excitement should've hit me by now. But it hasn't fully. Not until I know if Fred got a sponsorship from one of the places he applied to.

"You've barely touched your lunch."

I blink at Tina on the stool beside me. I'd almost forgotten I'm sharing lunch with some colleagues. The smell of fried food and after-rain hangs in the air. I lift the chapati wrapped in newspaper. "It's cold."

Tina tips her head toward the canteen where the man is still flipping chapati on a steamy pan. "It wasn't cold when you got it."

"If you don't eat it, I'll take it." Michael, sitting across from us, pats his stomach.

My phone buzzes in my pocket, and anticipation rises. It's Gertrude—Fred. "Here." I stand, handing Michael the chapati. "It's all yours." Then I rush toward the bushes surrounding the courtyard. "Fred?" I answer breathlessly.

"Hello."

Uh-oh. His voice sounds low and flat.

My stomach tightens. "You got the results?"

"Yeah."

I hold my breath.

He sighs, the sound crackling through the connection. "Didn't go the way I hoped."

My heart sinks. "Fred—what do you mean?"

"I'm not getting the sponsorship. Scores were good... but not good enough. You heard your father. Top five percent in the country are guaranteed the sponsorship."

Guaranteed wasn't exactly what Papa said, but that must've been the way Fred took it. I duck as a bee hovers closely, probably ready to dive into the flowers on the shrub.

"Tell me your scores." Clearly good enough for some institutes to take him.

"I did wonders in Astronomy and Geography and Divinity and Language thanks to you." He rattles them off mechanically. "Economics gets me out of the pool of qualifiers."

"Fred... that's not bad. That's really not bad."

"Not bad *if* you have the money to pay your own school fees." He huffs. "You know what I thought? I thought I'd surprise you. Be the man who gets a letter from the university or institute with my name on it in bold. Walk up to where you're working and say, 'Guess who made it?'"

I close my eyes, his disappointment sinking into my chest. "You did make it in my eyes. You left the village and managed *six years* of studying in *one year*. Fred, I'm so proud of—"

"No," he cuts me off, his voice sharp. "I'm still here. Still with my father locking me out of the land. Still selling cassava and avoiding a marriage I never wanted. Now, even the dream of learning is slipping away."

Papers rustle. He's probably crumpling his results letter.

"Please don't tell me you're crunching that paper up?"

He draws out a dreadful sigh. "No, I didn't."

"Good."

"It was good to dream while I could."

"We'll figure it out. And maybe one of the institutes will contact you, even if your results don't meet the scholarship requirements."

"That's not going to happen."

He's right. I shift my left foot over my right. "There are private institutions, cheaper ones. I can ask around. I can talk to—"

"Lucy." His tone turns me cold. "You said it's going to take plenty of years for you to become a doctor."

"Six years." My words die in my throat. Of course, he remembers everything I told him about my career path.

"You'll be in clinics. Hospitals." Each word comes through heavier than the last. "And I'll still be here... waiting."

His question hangs between us, a shadow I can't chase away. Is he giving up on us?

"I know it's a long wait." I can barely force my voice above a whisper. "I know I have no promises to give, but I also don't want you to feel obligated to wait for me." I swallow hard, searching for words. "If it's of any comfort, I told you we should get married one time, remember?"

His laugh is bitter. "Yeah, and if we had, your father would have disowned you, and you'd be here with me in the village, without land and a home to call our own."

"We can always buy our own land. Land isn't that expensive in the village."

"It is expensive. For me, anyway."

"I can help contribute." My voice sounds small even to my ears.

"You're missing the point, Lucy," he snaps, making me flinch.

"Then what is the point?" My body heats up as my frustration rises. "Tell me."

"I want to be someone who deserves you." His voice cracks. "Someone who can stand beside you as an equal, not as the charity case who needed your family's help."

My lips part, my response trapped behind the lump in my throat. "Yes, our families come from different worlds, but we can either dwell on that and stay stuck or do something about it and become who we want to be."

"If I can't further my studies and I just marry you, your father stops paying for you because of me. How can I live with that?"

"We'll figure it out. Let's take one step at a time." I pour every ounce of conviction I have into those words, but it's probably not enough to ease Fred's discouragement.

"Goodbye, Lucy."

Then the line goes dead, and the phone beeps, ending our conversation.

I clutch the phone, staring at the screen, hoping he'll call back and say he isn't ready to give up on his dreams.

Yes, our backgrounds are different. I have parents who worry about my future, who fund my studies and pave the way. Fred? He's chasing his dreams alone. But he has me.

I press the phone to my chest, helpless. I can't comfort him from miles away.

Then I tap the phone against my chin. An idea begins to spiral. Maybe I can convince Papa that I need another break to visit Mama in the village? With my siblings back in school, she could use the company.

It's not like I'm being paid to be here. Asking for time off from the hospital shouldn't be hard.

Fred needs me.

CHAPTER 13

THE WORLD SHAKES

Fred

The metal shelves in Gertrude's shop creak under new inventory. I stack clear jars of nails in rows along one.

"No, not like that." John calls from across the shop. He rounds the counter, pointing. "Those go with the hinges and screws. Customer logic, Fred. If they're buying nails, they'll probably need those too."

Makes sense. I shift the jars to the shelf he pointed at. I still don't understand how a hardware-slash-fabric store is supposed to be organized. John walked me through it earlier, but my head isn't in it today. Hasn't been since that call with Lucy almost a week ago.

"You're distracted." John leans against the counter. "Still thinking about those exam results?"

"No," I lie, then sigh. "Yes. And Lucy."

Hard not to think of her here. This shop has become the closest thing to her—where I get to hear her voice, even if just through a phone line. "I wish I could make things right with her."

"You will." John claps me on the back, then moves to tighten the rope coiled around a metal hook near the bolts and chains.

I called Lucy two days after our last conversation. There was no answer. I waited an hour, tried again—nothing. She's upset, and she has every right to be.

Gertrude, John's wife, told me to come back today. She said she'd reach out to Lucy and arrange a time for us to talk. So now, I'm here waiting for Lucy's call.

"Stay for supper." John hooks another thick rope onto a U-shaped peg above the shelf. "Gertrude made your favorite—groundnut sauce and mushroom. This time with matooke."

I rarely eat matooke. I should say no. But the smell drifting from the back door—warm, earthy—makes my stomach growl loud enough to shame me.

Food shouldn't be on my mind right now. But here I am.

"Guess I'll wait for that call."

"Good." John's eyes twinkle with something I can't quite read. "Before I forget—I spoke with the new assistant principal yesterday."

My attention snaps into focus. "About what?"

"I found a place for your sister to stay if she comes next term." He beams. "If she's willing to cook and clean the teachers' homes, one of the female teachers agreed to host her."

My stomach tightens. I picture the senior math teacher, the one who looks my age. I scratch at my barely-there beard. "I'm not sure I want her near the single male teachers' quarters."

"Good point. We thought of that. I've got daughters—I get it." He nods. "Only married teachers. She'll clean when both husband and wife are home. And female teachers. So far, three are interested." He smiles. "And the one who's offered to take her in is a kindhearted grandmother."

"Mrs. Mawire?"

He nods.

Wow. The widow treats everyone like her own—from staff to students, even me when I was just the gardener.

"Really?" Hope flares in my chest, something I haven't felt in weeks. "Mr. Lugire, that would be—" I choke back the lump rising in my throat. "That would change everything. For her. For my family."

"Your sister deserves the same opportunity you got. And from what you've told me, she's even brighter than you."

"Oof, what a blow." I feign a wince, then laugh. It's true. She reads books I wouldn't have touched at her age. "She is. But Mama needs—"

"Your parents need their children to do something more," he cuts in. "Not just to fetch water and plow fields all their lives."

A man in dusty work clothes strides through the wide double doors, nodding at both of us. "I need ten kilos of nails. Rain season. My house doesn't need the clouds' permission to fall apart."

John chuckles as he heads for the shelves. "Coming right up."

I keep organizing the shelves, but my mind is half with Lucy and half with the possibility of her future. One path opens, another threatens to close.

My chest aches with the thought of losing her. I shouldn't have called her when I was a jumble of emotions. If she doesn't call back today, I'll have to find her in the city. The only issue? I wouldn't even know where to start. Maybe this is how life balances itself—giving and taking all at once.

The customer leaves, and John returns to our earlier conversation.

"What will you tell your sister?"

The door creaks open, louder this time, followed by voices I barely register. I stay focused, aligning the last row of nail packets, when—

"Excuse me, Mr. Lugire," a familiar voice says. "I'm looking for someone."

My heart stops.

I turn, a packet of nails frozen in my grip.

Lucy.

Neat rows of braided hair fall over her shoulders like woven silk over her yellow dress—the same one she wore that Sunday I watched her from behind the mango tree. And in her eyes, that same look, like she's weathered storms and come out standing taller.

My lips part. I'm not even sure they're mine. I can't find the words. "What are you...?"

"I had to see you."

My throat tightens. I shake my head, eyes stinging.

"I... wished..." Everything in the shop blurs as Lucy moves forward, sharpening my focus. She's real. Not the ghost I imagine whenever that song "Ghost" plays. It's my go-to when I miss her most.

"I hope it's okay that I came." She sets her handbag on the supply table.

The packet slips from my hand. I step around the shelf and close the distance, pulling her into my arms. I breathe in her scent—Lucy and only Lucy—mingled by the subtle perfume in her braids as they brush against my shoulder. The words catch in my throat, barely making it out. "You came back."

"You were upset." Her breath warms my neck as she squeezes me tight.

"I'm sorry. I shouldn't have put my grievances on you."

"You should do just that."

When we part, Lucy turns to John, who stands to the side, watching with amused eyes.

"Oh, young love." He shakes his head.

"Thank you." Lucy reaches for her handbag and pulls something out. She hands it to him—a plaque. "For believing in him."

John studies it, grinning. "No thanks needed." He turns it over, nodding. "Custom-made. Thank you."

Then he angles it toward me. "This boy has talents that shouldn't go to waste. Now, come, both of you. Supper's ready."

As we follow him, I lean close to Lucy. "Did you plan this?"

She smiles, her fingers brushing mine. "Gertrude might've helped. A little."

In the small dining area behind the shop, Gertrude sets plates piled high on the wooden table. Her face lights up when she spots Lucy.

"There she is! Right on time!" She hugs Lucy. "I told you he'd be here stacking things. The boy never stops working."

Lucy laughs. "Thank you for arranging this. For calling me back."

"When Fred said you weren't answering, I knew something was off." Gertrude shoots me a look. "Men think silence solves problems. Women know better."

"I tried calling," I mumble.

"After breaking her heart." She hands Lucy a plate. "Sometimes 'I'm sorry' needs to be said face-to-face, not down a wire."

John clears his throat. "Let's eat before the food gets cold. Let's talk while we eat."

Over the meal, Lucy shares stories from her hospital internship—procedures, patients, the way the ward smells at sunrise. Her hands move as she talks, full of life.

I can't stop watching her. Still can't believe she's here. She came all this way... for me.

"And what about you, Fred?" Gertrude's voice pulls me back. "I hope you have some new plans to further your education. Care to update Lucy?"

Across the table, Lucy's eyes find mine. Not pity or disappointment from our last conversation. Yes, I'd been so discouraged, but after thinking it through, I realized I couldn't just end all the work I put in last year.

"Teaching is still on the table. Just need to work out some details."

"One step at a time," John says. "You and Lucy have a lot to talk about."

Lucy decides not to go to her family. "I'll go tomorrow. I just want us to talk without sneaking around."

Her voice floats like music on my back as I pedal the bicycle, her arms resting lightly on the sides of the passenger seat.

"What do you have in mind?"

"The hill tonight."

"Is that why you bought blankets and a torch from Gertrude?"

"How did you not figure that out sooner?"

My heart warms. The energy pulsing through me as I pedal over hill after hill is something I haven't felt in a long time.

We reach our hill as daylight disappears. Then we lie on the blanket, her head on my shoulder—familiar and right. The moon hangs bright above us, the sky clear, no clouds in sight.

She laces her fingers through mine. "Tell me everything."

And I do.

I tell her about the day the results came—How my hands shook as I unfolded the paper. How I'd hoped the numbers might change if I looked at the paper hard enough. How I walked for hours afterward, not ready to go home.

I tell her about my father, how he laughed when he heard. "What did you expect?" he said. "All that time you wasted."

I tell her about the nights I've spent wondering what comes next. About what John said—about the place for Viola. "A part of me feels like maybe I shouldn't drag Viola into learning."

"There's a chance for her to go to school. We have to take it."

The "we" in her response captures my attention. Like we already belong in each other's worlds, even without rings or vows. My heart stumbles, and doubt creeps in. I have nothing to offer her. Even if I become a teacher in the village, the reward won't be much—some crops from the harvest maybe, but not money. Not anything close to what she deserves.

"Everyone has something to fall back on—land, money, family. I have none of that."

"You have me." She squeezes my hand. "We have each other. God has us. That should be enough."

"God. You." My lips curl. "Yeah... I should be okay, I guess."

"You guess?" She bumps my elbow.

I feign a wince and rub the spot before tucking my arm around her.

"You think I'm going to become some doctor overnight?" She snuggles in. "I don't even know if I'll regret giving up my boutique dream. But after Cutie died, I just... I thought maybe it'd be good to have doctors around here."

My heart jumps. Is she saying she might come back as a doctor in Busobi?

"I wouldn't want to live in this village forever." She answers my question before I ask. "But my sister's death compelled me to change careers. The unknown might be wonderful... or not. But we can't stop dreaming. Can't just walk away from everything we built."

I look at her through the soft filter of moonlight. The girl whose dreams gave me permission to dream. Because of her, I went back to school. "Even if I never continue with my education, you've helped me reach further than I ever imagined."

She breathes out, shifts beside me, then nudges my shoulder until I turn. Now we're face-to-face under the night sky.

"God didn't bring you this far to leave things unfinished. You have a destination, Fred. And you're not there yet. Do you even want to continue studying?"

After everything I've explored through learning? "I'm more eager now than ever. School gave me a hunger I didn't know I had."

"Then our next step is to pray. Ask God to make a way where there doesn't seem to be one."

"You sound so much like your mama... in a good way."

"Spiritual, you mean?"

"I like your sudden confidence in the faith."

"Mama took us to church at Christmas. I still remember the pastor's message about believing in the impossible. He said something I wrote in my diary." She pauses, eyes shining. "Your path doesn't define you. God's grace refines you."

The words sink in.

"Someday I want to go back to that church." She tucks her elbow under her, rising a bit. "Maybe with a testimony that God changed the impossible."

Maybe I could go with you. Maybe someday God will rewrite my story too. I want to say that. But right now, my future's still fogged in.

We fall quiet, staring up at the stars.

I'm just thankful the sky didn't open up with rain tonight. Otherwise, we wouldn't be here like this. She'd be at her house. I'd be alone in my hut.

Maybe God does care for me, after all.

CHAPTER 14

THE DAYS WE HAVE

Fred

The next day, I ride Lucy back into town, and we take our time, stretching every moment we can.

We eat rice, matooke, and chicken stew at one of the canteens I supply produce to. No bill needed—it's an even trade.

We wander through the market, holding hands. I introduce her to the vendors who run the fruit stands, the grain sacks, the cracked-wood counters where I've left my harvest more times than I can count.

At midafternoon, we start heading back, taking the long way home. We stop on hilltops to catch our breath, laughing about nothing and everything.

"I have to go home and say hello to Mama," she says as afternoon stretches toward evening. "Pretend like we haven't seen each other yet. I'll have a different bicyclist take me from here on."

I stop at the village between ours and Gertrude's and rest my hand on her shoulder. I wish I could be the one taking her, but we both know we can't announce our reunion to half the village yet. "I'll hover behind the trees while you catch a ride. Just to make sure it's someone safe."

"I don't remember this village having kidnappers."

I shrug. "Let's stick to elderly cyclists. Ones not in the market for a wife."

She laughs, but we both know anyone would think twice before crossing the officer's daughter. Still, money talks. A few coins and a bike ride is worth the risk to some.

"If you want, come help Mama with chores tomorrow." Her eyes gleam with their familiar mischief. "Then we can spend the whole day together."

"Don't they go gardening tomorrow?"

"If you show up early enough, maybe you'll join us. I know you have to garden too—"

"Mine can wait." Being cut off doesn't mean I can't still help my mother and siblings. I've even still been able to sell some of the produce I've grown on Father's land. "You're only here for a few more days." And I'm the reason she returned.

My heart pounds at the thought of seeing her again. The night stretches too long as I toss and turn, sleep refusing to come.

At the first rooster crow, I'm out of bed and pedaling toward her house. I hover by the creek, waiting.

When I spot Edna gathering wood behind the kitchen, I wait until she disappears inside before making my way to the house, my heart climbing into my throat.

Primrose answers the door. Her eyes narrow, suspicion flickering behind them. "Fred." My name lands somewhere between a greeting and a question. "What brings you here?"

I clear my throat, holding onto the excuse we rehearsed. "Good morning, madam. I was wondering if you had any trees that need clearing or maybe wood to split."

It's not the first time I've shown up early looking for work, but it's been a few days.

"I always have work." The corners of her mouth twitch. Then she calls over her shoulder. "Lucy! You have a visitor."

Lucy steps out, her surprise a little too practiced. "Fred! What a surprise!"

"Your lucky day—Lucy's here." Primrose practically rolls her eyes. She glances at me again, amusement and suspicion tugging at her expression. "You sure you're not here for Lucy?"

I meet her gaze. Steady. Honest.

"I'm here to help, madam. School fees... whatever you need."

Primrose sighs, but steps aside. "Since you're here, I've got sacks of beans that need moving to the food barn. Either that, or you can start filling sacks with maize. The harvesters left the job half done after shelling the cobs."

"Mama, can I help Fred instead of going to the garden with you?" Lucy tilts her head, pleading. "Please?"

Primrose shakes her head, but she's smiling. "As long as you don't distract each other. I need the job done."

"We won't."

I gulp a swallow, still surprised she trusts me enough to leave us alone.

The officer made it clear—*stay away from Lucy, don't come close.* Primrose doesn't approve either. But maybe she thinks Lucy won't take someone like me seriously—a farmer, a dreamer without much to offer.

Still, she makes it easier to be near Lucy. And for that, I'm grateful.

Even more so later, when she insists I stay for lunch.

I should give Lucy my full attention, but with the ground still soft, I need to plow before the rainy season comes to an end. I'm not sure what Lucy tells her mama the next morning, but somehow, she convinces Primrose to let Lucy follow me when I borrow the oxen. She walks beside me into the fields—land that stretches wide and rich, but which, according to my father, I have no right to unless I marry Safiri.

At least my siblings still have a claim. My mother too. They're the reason I keep showing up, doing what needs to be done. Of course, my father wouldn't forbid me to work.

The oxen move steadily, cutting clean furrows through the soil. I guide the two bulls with practiced ease. "I'm grateful your mama still lets us use her oxen."

I steal a glance at Lucy, the blue sky behind her, midmorning sunlight catching in her braids, and my heart soars.

The oxen veer off course. I scramble to correct them.

"You're hopelessly in love," she teases. "I've seen you plow straighter rows with your eyes closed."

"My eyes are open now." I mean more than just the work. "And I see what matters."

She bumps my shoulder. "Focus, farmer. Or we'll be here till midnight."

"Would that be so terrible?"

"Not at all." She smiles through her response, and it does something to my chest.

We fall into a rhythm—her in step nearby, the oxen leading, the land parting clean. With her here, even the labor feels lighter. I catch myself whistling—something I haven't done in months.

During a water break, she hands me the jug, watching me with thoughtful eyes. "I like seeing you like this. Like the Fred I remember."

"I'm still him. Just... weathered."

"Weathered things last longer." She bats her long eyelashes. "They know how to bend without breaking."

We make plans to go hunting with my friends the next evening. The rest of the day passes too fast. I don't see her much the next day, but that evening, we head to meet up with the guys.

"I can't wait to see Aisha. I need to hear all about married life." Lucy shifts her camera, snapping a photo of a critter skittering across the path.

"Don't get your hopes up. I'm not sure Kawo will bring her along."

"Didn't you tell him I was coming?"

"I did."

We reach the gathering spot where my friends are waiting. Aisha sees Lucy and runs straight into her arms.

Henry raises a brow as they pull apart. "You're bringing her? To hunt?"

Lucy flashes a sweet smile, lifting her hands. "Aisha and I will be off taking pictures while you men stalk the brush. Don't worry. We won't scare off the game with our feminine presence."

Henry chuckles, shaking her hand. "Good to see you again, Lucy. And good to see Fred smiling for once."

We head into the bush, the grass crunching underfoot. Lucy and Aisha fall back, arms linked, laughter drifting through the trees behind us.

"I don't want Aisha thinking she's tagging along every time now," Kawo grumbles.

"You've been leaving her home for weeks. You know she came for Lucy."

Henry leans close, voice dropping. "You're still pursuing her? Even after the results?"

"I didn't fail."

"What's the difference?"

"The difference is I passed, just not high enough for a sponsor. Without money, I'm stuck."

Henry eyes me, thoughtfully. "So what now? Where do you go from here?"

A branch snaps under my foot. "I don't know yet. But I'm not giving up. Lucy believes in me."

"Lucy..." He tests her name on his tongue. "I'm guessing the officer doesn't know she's here with you?"

"Her father knows."

"But not this part." Kawo grins.

I nod, and pride creeps into my voice. "She came for me."

"She's one fierce woman," Henry says.

"A wild one," Kawo adds.

When I raise my slingshot toward him, he waves his hands. "In a good way, I mean."

Henry nudges me. "She must really love you."

"And I love her too."

It's been four days together. Another night under the stars with the telescope she gave me a year ago. During the day, we sit by the creek near her home. We talk for hours, sharing ideas about where I can apply, where she might find work between semesters. I write down every suggestion in the diary she gifted me, treating her words the way I should the gospel.

We talk about teaching colleges within taxi distance of her nursing school, about part-time jobs I could take while studying, about dreams that suddenly feel within reach.

With Lucy here, I can breathe again. The future doesn't feel so impossible.

"We'll make it work," she promises on our second-to-last night, her determination catching fire in my chest. "One term at a time if we have to."

For the first time in months, I believe it. I'm back to believing in myself again too.

CHAPTER 15

THE MAMAS

Lucy

I need a plan for Fred before I leave. I'll have to utilize my after-supper conversation with Mama before bedtime to see if this will work.

As I follow her to her bedroom, the quiet house feels strange without even the boys around. Even Ivan started kindergarten this year. I did fine at their age in boarding school, but their mischief might land them in trouble.

"Do you ever get lonely now that all the kids are in school?" I set the lamp on Mama's bedside table. Framed photos crowd the surface—Mama and Papa on their wedding day, my siblings and I through the years.

"You ask me that with only one day left here. That doesn't help my case."

She sits in the center of the bed, and I slide beside her, the mattress dipping under my weight. Even with my time spent with Fred, Mama and I carved out slow hours to sew tablecloths.

Now, she reaches for my hand. "I was so sure this was where God wanted me to be." Her gaze drifts to the wire across the room where a few clean clothes hang drying.

"After discovering all those churches in the city—ones we don't have here—I've found myself hungry for more of God. That fire. That faith again."

"I know."

If Mama moves, I won't have a strong excuse to visit the village. But I get it. Now that she's not raising the kids here, she no longer has much reason to stay so far from Papa.

"If I move to Mukono, I could go to church any day I want. I could visit your siblings on visitation weekends. Then during the holidays, we'd all return to the village together."

"Have you told Papa?"

"Not exactly. I'm praying about it."

I lean my head on her shoulder. "I'll pray with you, Mama." Then I add what I've been thinking. "If we find someone we trust to take care of the house while we're gone, manage the workers, keep an eye on the stock, it could work."

"I think so too, my darling child." She untangles our hands and rubs a gentle circle on my back. "What are your plans for Fred?"

"Mama." I stifle a laugh, trying to play it off. But Mama knows already. I swing my feet on the cool cement. "I still like him."

"I know. That poor boy... I'm not sure he can afford to continue with school, but I admire his determination."

I lift my head away from her shoulder. "I want to ask Papa if he can help Fred get into a teaching institute. Papa knows a lot of people, and he's worked in so many cities. Surely, he knows someone who leads an institute. And even if he doesn't, people listen when he speaks."

The lamp casts its soft glow across her face. "I agree." She tucks my braids behind my ear. "Your father knows people. And he's good at presenting himself anywhere. But Fred can't afford college fees."

"We're not rich." I draw out a slow breath. "But by village standards, we're the wealthiest. Even in the city, we're doing fine." I dare not push too hard, but Papa listens to her. "The nursing school offered me housing, and Papa already paid for it. But what if I stayed outside the quarters? It's a lot cheaper off campus. Some of that money could go toward helping Fred."

She nods, her smile soft. "I'm not sure you'll convince your father to change your housing, but there's a chance he'll listen if you ask him to help Fred get into an institute. Fred must have enough saved up to get him started."

I try not to think about how much it'll cost—school fees, housing, supplies. Step one is talking to Papa.

"Do you think he'll listen to me? About Fred?"

"He understands the value of education. He was the only one in his family who went to school." Her eyes narrow. "But don't involve your feelings for Fred when you talk to him about this."

"I won't."

Of course, I'll still push for institutes and universities close to my nursing school. Twenty minutes apart at most.

"Your father watches," Mama says, like she's reading my mind. "He sees more than he says."

"Is that good or bad?"

"That depends on what he's seeing." Her smile is enigmatic. "Before you talk to him, visit the pastor at that church in Mukono. Ask him to pray with you, so God can make a way. Maybe write a letter too, explaining everything."

There are churches closer to where Papa works, but Mukono is only a thirty-minute taxi ride away. I could stop there on my way back to Kampala.

I'm desperate for a miracle for Fred. And right now, only God can do it.

Eager to tell Fred what I discussed with Mama, I barely manage a quick shower the next morning after farmwork before rushing to the creek—an hour earlier than we'd planned.

He's already there.

We walk through the wide-open land on our property, aimlessly. I tell him everything I spoke to Mama about—the possible institute and university options, the housing costs, the unknowns we might face.

Clouds stretch across the sky, heavy with the promise of rain. Like there's hope hanging there too, if everything works out.

"Two of the institutes you applied to could still work." I pause to untangle my dress from a gnarly shrub.

He stays quiet. Too quiet.

I squeeze his hand. "What do you think of all this?"

He stops as the path widens. His breath is slow. Shoulders slumped. "How am I supposed to show up in front of your father? He already doesn't like me. And now I'm supposed to come to him as a beggar?"

"You're not a beggar." The words come out too sharp. "Please don't go down the self-pity road."

"Easy for you to say." He yanks a leaf from a shrub and tosses it aside, avoiding my eyes. "You have school lined up. School fees paid. Your future doesn't depend on begging someone who despises you." He then brings up the old tension between our families. The history neither of us asked for.

My chest tightens. The truth in his words hurts more than any lie ever could.

"It's not fair to keep dragging the past into what the future could be."

"But it is what it looks like. You're leaving tomorrow, moving forward. And I'm still here, begging my father for soil to stand on."

"So what?" I suck in a breath and blink back the sting. Anger rises fast, hot. "You want me to stay stuck until you catch up?"

His eyes flash. "That's not what I said."

"But it's what you feel."

I brush past him, storming through the trees, ignoring the scratches on my shins as the thorns rip through my skirt. Why didn't I wear shorts?

"Lucy, wait!" His footsteps pound the earth behind me. "I just want us to have something solid. I can't offer you anything while my dreams are still buried in the dirt."

I spin to face him, heat rising through every inch of me. "I've never given you a reason to think I want your money. I just want your heart, Fred."

"And you have my heart." He looks away, jaw tight. "But I don't want you carrying my problems like they're yours."

"Why can't I?" Isn't that what love is? "When you're hurting, I hurt too. When your dreams fall apart, mine do too. Can't you see that?"

"I see it." His voice drops. "That's why I want you to focus on you. Don't let me be the reason your father pulls his support." He takes a breath. "We both need to breathe. Don't do anything yet. Please."

"Fine."

We walk in silence. At this point, we're not even sure where we're headed—and I don't mean just for our walk.

The path bends around a cluster of banana trees. Then we're not alone. A group of women appears ahead, balancing jerricans on their heads, returning from the well. Not the pump. This is the one used after the rainy season before it dries up.

One woman narrows her eyes at me.

Oh, great. Fred's mother. The others murmur greetings and pass by, but she stops steps away.

Fred halts beside me.

His mother glares. Then she lifts the jerrican off her head and sets it on the ground. "Shouldn't you be in the city?"

"I will be tomorrow." Not that I owe her an explanation, but with the history between our families, maybe I do.

She plants a hand on her hip. Her long black dress is torn along the hem. Given my recent encounter with gnarly branches, I imagine it's hard to keep a dress intact while wandering in the bushes.

"You."

Just one word has me looking at her. Her disdainful expression chills me. I want my mama. But she's not here.

I square my shoulders. His mother's a stranger, and I won't have her intimidating me.

"Because of you, my son isn't married. Because of you, my husband won't stay in my house. Because of you, my daughter asks questions no girl should ask. Because of you, I stand alone at the well while the other women whisper."

As she relays the problems I've caused his family, each one strikes like a hammer to stone.

Fred steps forward. "Mama, please don't."

She doesn't even look at him as she continues.

I bite the inside of my cheek to keep from opening my mouth. The temptation is high, escalating, and I'm not sure how long I can keep up. I even hold my breath as if letting it out will be my undoing.

"Leave Fred alone." She points a finger at me. "You've done enough damage."

"Fred is an adult." I'm not sure how my lips parted, saying what needs to be said. "He makes his own choices." I shift my foot from side to side, heat bubbling beneath my stomach.

Fred rests his hand on my lower back, maybe to silence me.

It's time to end whatever this is. Head high, I face her. "I think you've said enough."

"Fred! You see how disrespectful she is? She talks to your mama like that when you're not even married?" Her voice cracks, nostrils flaring, eyes burning holes through me. "You are not worth my son's love."

"Mama, enough!" Fred steps in front of me, his hand falling away from my waist.

I sidestep him and lift my chin toward his mother. "You think you're worthy of your husband's love when he's married to two other women? Chances are, he spends more time with his younger wives than you." I spit. "Funny how you blame me for it. Was I the one who told him to marry other women?"

"Lucy, stop it!"

His voice cuts through me. When I look at him, his eyes blaze. He confirms who it's geared to when he tosses his hands and glowers at me. "You don't have to say everything that comes into your head! It won't solve anything."

Wait. *I'm* the one he's scolding? I blink. "So it's okay for your mother to throw accusations, but I can't defend myself?"

"That's not what I—"

"I'm done with you and your family."

I turn before I say more, before I unravel. I don't care about helping Fred anymore. Grass crunches beneath my flats as I storm off.

His voice chases me. "Lucy! Wait!"

"Fred!" his mother cries out.

"Lucy!" he calls again.

I whirl around, hands fisting. "Leave me alone."

"I'll walk you home."

"I'm capable of walking by myself." I spit the words like poison. "Go back to your mother. She needs you more than I do right now."

I walk faster, tears blurring my vision. One drops onto my arm. I swipe it away like it offends me.

A giant rat steps into my path. I jump, screaming, and the rat leaps back into the bushes.

My heart thunders so loud. The sky has darkened. It could rain any moment. A slight fear creeps in. What if I get lost?

The path feels twice as long. My thoughts spiral with every word I could've said—and the ones I shouldn't have.

"I can't stand any of you!" I scream into the trees, my voice tearing through the tight lump in my throat.

How dare Fred's parents treat him like a child? But even more, how dare he not choose me when it counted, not stand with me while his mother verbally attacked me.

"What's the point of fighting for you"—my voice breaks—"when you won't even fight for me?"

Hot tears slip down my cheeks. I swipe them away and kick at a lump of dirt. It's soft, and mud seeps into the side of my shoe.

Through my blurred vision, the sight of the creek brings relief. I follow it home, step after heavy step. By the time I reach the stretch where it cuts through our property, my legs ache, and my chest feels like it's caving in.

I drop to the bank, knees pulled in, gaze on the water. The recent rain swelled the creek's waters, the current tugging fallen leaves downstream. The surface nearly brushes the wide, flat rocks that form a crossing.

I blow out of my mouth, steadying my breath. Maybe my departure tomorrow will fix everything.

I'll return to the city. Forget Fred—like I should've the moment our eyes met on the church grounds over a year ago.

But the thought carries a sadness I can't shake.

Every step forward now will cost me something. And this time, it's him.

I'm not sure I can carry the weight of that kind of loss. Or maybe I can—and that's why the sky splits open, releasing the downpour I've been holding inside. I run home as the first drops turn to sheets of rain. By nightfall, it's pouring, soaking the earth and changing it into clinging mud.

It's going to be a rough bike ride into town tomorrow. I hope our herdsman knows how to handle the road.

CHAPTER 16

WHEN IT'S HER WHO SAVES US

Fred

It always takes me too long to make the right decision. Not like Lucy. She acts fast. And somehow, always sure she made the right call.

I sink the hoe beneath the weeds into damp earth, yawn, and dig again. I started at five this morning, wanting to stay close to home until daylight. Now the sun is rising, burning off last night's rain. Maybe it'll stay dry long enough for Lucy to ride safely into town.

The herdsman was supposed to take her like he ferries her half siblings.

But my heart sinks with every swing of the hoe. Lucy's slumped figure replays in my mind. That's not how I thought our last day would end.

I'd pictured holding her hand as we walked together, laughing, picking flowers—doing everything and nothing. Instead, I argued.

Then I remained silent when Mama spoke so rudely. I couldn't disrespect Mama by defending Lucy.

I stayed behind, watching from a distance to make sure she got home. Lucy was scared of that rodent on the path, but she bounced back fast like she always does. But hearing her cry—hearing her yell about me, my family—tore something inside me.

My hands go stiff on the handle, her voice echoing through my skull. "I can't stand any of you! ... What's the point of fighting for you?"

I'm the reason she cried, the reason she's mad, *and* the reason she came back in the first place.

She's right. I didn't stand up for her. If the roles were reversed, if it were her father putting me in my place, she would've spoken up without hesitation.

"Fred! Fred!" Viola's panicked voice snaps me out of my thoughts. She wheezes through the fruit trees, and fear etches her frown. "Quick!"

I drop the hoe and sprint toward the house, mud sucking at my bare feet. Shoes are useless on the ground like this.

"What's wrong?" My heart pounds against my ribs. Viola never sounds like that unless it's serious.

"Mama!" Her voice cracks as she races back.

I break into a run.

The scene inside freezes my blood. Mama is hunched over in her chair, hands pressed hard to her stomach, her face twisted in pain. Sweat beads on her forehead. She's breathing like each inhale costs her everything.

My younger siblings look terrified. I steer them outside. No reason they should see Mama like this.

"What happened?" I kneel beside her.

A small saucepan sits on the stove I bought six months ago to make morning cooking easier.

"She was making porridge." Viola wrings her hands. "She dropped the spoon and bent over like this. Then she said it felt like burning fire in her side. It came out of nowhere."

Mama groans, her fingers digging into her abdomen. "My right side," she whispers. "It's like something's tearing inside."

Panic slams into my chest. "Get the bicycle ready. Now."

Viola rushes out.

I turn to Mama. Somehow, I even keep my voice steady. "We're going to the clinic. Can you stand?"

She kinda nods.

The nearest clinic, almost an hour away, only sells medicine. If she needs surgery, we'll have to go all the way to the bigger town—near Gertrude's shop.

Will Mama even make it that far? Even if we get there, can I count on them to treat her right away? That clinic serves several villages. It's always busy.

What choice do I have?

We fly down the muddy dirt path. Every bump makes Mama groan, and I pedal harder, heart pounding louder than the tires slamming into rock.

Her fingers clutch my waist, anchoring herself as I push forward.

The officer's house comes into view, and so does Lucy in my mind.

She's smart. Maybe not a doctor yet, but she's been reading, watching operations. She might be Mama's best chance if she hasn't already left.

"Almost there."

Doubts swarm like mosquitoes. What if our fight cut her too deep? What if she won't help?

But Lucy is kind.

I breathe out, whispering a prayer. "Let her be there, God. She said You do the impossible. This is one of those times. Please... let her be there. And let her know what to do."

There really is a God of miracles because I spot the herdsman walking toward the cow stable.

"I need help!" I shout, braking hard. Mama's hands are still tight around my waist as she groans.

He rushes over.

"Is Lucy still around?"

"She slept in—we missed the bus."

I let out a breath. I don't even have to ask. He's already moving to the back of the bicycle.

The older man steadies Mama as I slide off the seat. "What's wrong with your mother?"

"I was hoping Lucy might have some answers. She's been watching the doctors... learning things."

Already, we're carrying Mama toward the house.

Primrose, as if she's been watching, pushes the door open, then steps aside. "What's wrong?"

I explain while she calls for Edna to bring a blanket to the sitting room, where we lower Mama onto the floor.

"Maybe that's why God sent all this rain—so Lucy could stay." Primrose peers down the corridor. "Lucy! Come quickly!"

Lucy soon appears. Her eyes widen when she sees me. There's a flicker of something—hurt, maybe anger. Whatever it was, it vanishes the moment she sees Mama curled on the floor.

"What happened?" She drops to her knees beside Mama.

I explain again while she checks Mama's wrist, then the other. She counts her pulse, presses her fingers to Mama's stomach, and asks where it hurts as she moves from side to side with care. "I'll grab my medical bag."

While she hurries off, I pray it holds what she needs. She brought it after Christmas and left it behind, saying we could use it in case of emergencies.

"I saw this before." She kneels beside Mama again as she opens the bag. "Exactly this. During my observation in the abdominal ward."

She takes out gloves and a stethoscope. "Could be biliary colic—gallbladder spasm. Pain comes on fast but settles with the right help. We don't need a hospital for it if that's what it is."

She asks Mama a series of questions—the pain pattern, where it started, and how quickly it came on after eating. Then she names a few symptoms, and Mama nods in recognition.

"Those are classic signs of a gallbladder spasm." Lucy then looks around. "Edna, can you please warm up the rice bag and bring it?"

Edna nods and turns to leave.

"Also bring an iron," Lucy calls after her. "Add some hot coals."

"I'll go help Edna." Primrose disappears down the hallway.

"If it's colic, heat will ease the muscle spasm," Lucy explains.

My jaw nearly drops at her stunning calm, her confidence.

"The clinic wouldn't be able to do much more without proper equipment." She braces her hands on her knees. "What your mama needs right now is warmth and rest."

I figured they couldn't. Still, hearing it from her steadies something inside me.

She checks Mama's eyes for any yellowing. She says something about *jaundice*, and checking for signs of liver strain. Then she measures Mama's pulse again, fingers pressed to her wrist. "You're going to be alright."

There's no anger in her eyes. Just sympathy. Not for what happened between us, but for me, for my mother.

Primrose returns with the sewn fabric stuffed with rice. "Let's pray first."

We bow our heads. Her prayer is simple but strong, and when she ends with a soft amen, we echo it together.

Lucy lays the warm rice bag across Mama's lower right side, just under her ribs.

Mama exhales, some of the tension leaving her body.

When Edna returns with the iron wrapped in cloth, Lucy moves with quiet precision. She lays it in a metal pan. "I'll wrap it in cloth to protect her skin, then place it on her right side just below the ribs. Same spot the doctor showed me during that bowel obstruction procedure."

No doubt, Lucy can do anything she sets her mind to. That confidence alone—she's going to make a great doctor, wherever she ends up. Just the way she's holding Mama's hand, speaking in that same calm, steady tone—even after what happened yesterday—moves me.

Mama's still tense, but not as much. Her eyes, though filled with pain, watch Lucy with something close to hope.

"Help me arrange the cloths on the other side."

At Lucy's request, I move fast, and so does her mother.

We fold and stack the layers as instructed. Minutes pass. Mama's breathing shifts. Her jaw relaxes. The tension in her expression and tightness around her eyes eases like morning mist melting in the sun.

"It's going," she whispers. "The pain is going."

Relief rushes through me even more when Mama murmurs. "Lucy... I'm sorry. About yesterday."

"Today is a new day." Lucy squeezes her shoulder. "Everything is all right."

She then meets my eyes, calm, steady. And just like that, everything *is* all right.

"Let's take turns keeping the heat there for twenty minutes," she says. "Then remove it for ten, and—"

"I'll take a turn next," Primrose offers.

"Thanks, Mama." Lucy stands. "I'll get some water so she can stay hydrated."

"I'll come with you."

I follow her through the dining room and into the back room where they keep the clean cups, plates, and water pots. Then I finally look at my muddy feet, now dry, and the trail of footprints on the red cement floor. I'll have to clean their house before I leave.

Later.

Now, alone we're in the room, I take her hand, stop her, and turn her to face me. "I'm so sorry, Lucy."

"Your mom gave you a scare."

"But before that." I lift her fingers to my lips and kiss them. "I shouldn't have let Mama speak to you like that."

"It's your culture. I guess I need to—"

"It was wrong." I meet her eyes. "And while standing up to my parents—my father especially—is something I've learned, it's still new. But I'm getting there. Can you forgive me?"

Her chest rises and falls beneath her red and white polka dot blouse. She looks toward the window, at the curtain.

I squeeze her hand and place it over my chest. "Please. I'm terrified I hurt you deeply. Did you mean it when you said you were done with me?"

She snaps her gaze back to mine, blinking.

"Did you think I'd let you walk home alone? After we were already lost before we ran into my mama?"

She slaps my chest, a smile forming. "Glad you kept your distance. I'd have thrown a rock at your head."

"Which I'd have deserved. But a rock slap from you is fine—because you'd be the one nursing me back to health."

"How am I supposed to put up with you?" She closes the gap between us and wraps her arms around me.

We hold each other, hearts beating in silence.

"Thank you," I whisper. "For helping my mama."

"She'll still need to go to the hospital to get checked out." She exhales. "Honestly, I had no idea if any of that was going to work. But you trusted me, and I had to use what I had to make sure she was okay."

"That's why you'll make a great doctor someday."

"You'll make a great teacher, farmer, or whatever God wants you to be. It's not up to me to push you."

"I love you, Lucy."

I kiss her, sure and steady, and she kisses me back. The kiss deepens—until distant voices make us pull apart.

"I love you too." She steps back, turns to the drawer, and pulls out a glass. She fills the glass, using a plastic cup to ladle water from the pot.

Watching her, I know I'd do anything for her. Follow her anywhere. Because with her, I can be a better man. "I'd gladly accept any offer from your papa to help me get into school."

"Are you sure about that?"

"That's my best chance to see you often." I take the glass from her. "I'll follow you anywhere, Lucy."

She smiles. "Let's not forget—you have village kids to teach. For now, I guess you can follow me to the city."

With Mama resting, I offer to clean the muddy trail in the house, but Primrose suggests I split more wood instead.

"You don't have to pay me." I hint that her daughter already did more than enough by treating my mother.

I get to give Lucy a proper goodbye. We spend the day talking, laughing, like no hurt ever came between us.

Before she leaves, I ask Primrose. "Can I give Lucy a ride into town for her bus? It's the least I can do after everything you've all done for my mama."

"Yes, Mama," Lucy cuts in, wagging a playful finger at me. "He has to pay by carting me into town."

Primrose nods. "It's a very early departure. If you want to stay in our kitchen tonight—"

"I'll be here an hour early. I promise." Then I brave a teasing wink. "My bicycle lights are working perfectly."

Hours later, at home that night, Mama's breathing is heavy behind the curtain separating the sitting area from her bed. I'm guessing Father will stay the night in her hut.

The kerosene lamp flickers, lighting Viola's face as she shifts on the mat. My younger siblings sleep behind the curtain off to the side.

"If Lucy hadn't gone to school," I say into the quiet, "Mama might still be in pain. Or worse."

"Lucy is very smart." Viola says, "I want to be just like her when I grow up."

"Of course, you can't be like her," Father says. "She has money. You don't."

Viola's head lowers. "Maybe if I go to school..."

"Her knowledge saved your mother today." My father's words hang in the air like a shift in the wind. After a beat, he turns to me. "This school you want to go to, the teaching college. What would it cost?"

"A lot," I admit, though I'm not even sure what the fees are anymore. They've gone up since I last checked.

"I still have the north field. Not sure anyone in this village can afford it, but... it's all I can offer."

He doesn't say more. But he doesn't need to.

Is this it? Did he just... support me going to school?

Words lodge in my throat. I gape at him through the dim light, trying to read his face, but he isn't looking at me. Maybe he already regrets saying it.

"Thank you," I manage, voice rough.

He doesn't reply. But I'll cling to that hope.

It's been a good day, in the end. Mama's better. And tomorrow, I get to drive Lucy into town. Give her the goodbye she deserves. And is it possible I might be going to an institute?

CHAPTER 17

THE BIG REQUEST

Lucy

There's no time to spare. If I don't ask Papa today, I might never get the chance.

Warm light from the bulb spills through the kitchen as I ladle chicken stew over rice and cassava—Papa's portion generous, mine small. He ordered takeout for us, not wanting either of us to cook after my long trip back from the village. Now, the local news report drifts in from the sitting room where he waits for supper.

I stifle a yawn. I might turn in early tonight, even if I don't work tomorrow. Sundays are guaranteed rest days for me. For Papa too—though crime doesn't rest. There's always something, always a call dragging him back to the office.

It doesn't feel like Fred drove me on his bicycle to the bus station only hours ago—my arms wrapped around his waist, fingers feeling the taut muscles beneath his shirt as I breathed in the faint soapy scent of his skin. We hugged goodbye, not caring who stared.

Hugging isn't the norm in the village, but we held on, heartbeats syncing, tears sliding down our cheeks.

"I'll check the shop in town every other day." His voice caught as he kissed my cheek. "You call when you can."

I couldn't speak over the lump in my throat. I just nodded, sniffling against his chest.

The bus honked, clearly waiting on me. We pulled apart. His eyes were glassy, wet like mine.

"I love you, Lucy."

"I know." I bit my lip. It was all I could manage.

Right then, I decided to accomplish everything in one day. I got off the bus in Mukono, and I took a boda boda straight to the church office. The pastor prayed over me—over Fred. For God's favor. For courage. For Papa to understand when I spoke.

"How's supper coming?" Papa calls from the sitting room.

"Here it comes."

The TV clicks off. He's ready. As I step out of the kitchen, he heads to the dining table.

"Smells good," he says when I set the plate in front of him.

"Glad we got takeout. My cooking wouldn't smell that good."

"Don't underestimate yourself." He picks up his fork and slices into the bed of rice. "You cook supper for us almost every day now."

"True, but not the meat." I unfold the napkin on my lap, then suggest we pray.

He nods. When I finish, he adds his quiet amen. "Your mama's done a good job teaching you religion."

"She's teaching all of us." Including him. I now know that what Mama has is faith in God, rather than religion, but that's another conversation for another time.

I reach for my fork and take a bite. The sauce is rich with curry, garlic, and other spices. It melts in my mouth. I fork another bite. "Did you have any serious cases while I was gone?"

"If someone stealing another man's sheep counts..." He shrugs and continues with small theft cases—nothing heavy. No family disputes or domestic cases, the kind that dig deep for him. "How about you? Did you get enough rest?"

We'd already talked about my time in the village earlier. I reach for my glass and take a slow sip of water. I'll need it. This conversation isn't going to be easy. "I wanted to talk to you about Fred."

His fork clanks against the porcelain as he sets it down. His eyes widen, layered with emotions I can't quite read. "Don't tell me you're still running around with that boy."

"He helps Mama with some work. I ran into him at the well too."

Papa hadn't wanted Fred near our home since last year. But we shared a meal under the same roof, and no one threw any axes. Mama can defend herself if Papa questions her about letting Fred back in.

"He didn't get the sponsorship he hoped for."

"I expected as much."

My lips part, ready to defend Fred's intelligence, but I stop myself. One wrong tone, and this whole thing falls apart.

"He wants to become a teacher. You've worked in Kampala and neighboring towns for years. Maybe you know someone—an institute head or administrator who could help."

He narrows his gaze, exhales through his nose. Behind him, the painting of the national police force hangs crooked on the dining room wall. "Recommending him shouldn't be the problem. But where's he going to get the money?"

Relief spills through me. So he does know of some places.

"He's been selling crops. And, Papa, even though he didn't get sponsorship, he got very good results. Better than some students who've been in school their whole lives."

Papa nods as if thinking about it, then reaches for his chicken drumstick. "His father—"

"Actually, his father gave him land." I sit up straighter as I explain Fred's mama's health emergency and how I had to step in. When I'm done, I peek to see if he's been listening.

He leans back, his brows lifted in quiet disbelief. He then exhales, and his chest puffs out the worn T-shirt he favors when he's done with work. Is that pride I'm seeing?

"I'm sure word will get around in the village." A faint smile tugs at his mouth. "I always tell the elders the importance of education. Maybe now some people will understand."

"I think Fred's papa is finally understanding. One minute, he was sending Fred off his land. Next, he's offering him a piece of it."

"Unless someone trades him a cow for the land—one he can sell for cash in the main town—he'll have no other way to earn anything from it in the village."

"One step at a time, Papa." I shift on the wooden chair. "So... will you help him?"

"I'll make the call first thing Monday." He lifts his chicken to take a bite like he hasn't just shifted the course of two lives with one sentence. My life changes when Fred's does. "I know the chairman of the board at Kamura University on Jinja Road. I have to call in anyway for your friend, Molly, and her brother. But he better have the results to back it up."

"Thank you." I cover my mouth to hold in a squeal, so my next words come out muffled. "Thank you, Papa."

This is all God. Mama's prayers. The pastor's prayers? That's got to be the only reason Papa didn't question every detail about Fred. He didn't say anything about our relationship either. But he knows I still care for Fred, even though he made it clear Fred was to stay away from me and for me not even to consider a relationship with him. All that doesn't matter at the moment.

I scoop rice with my fork. Happiness drowns out the flavor. I can't wait to call Gertrude's shop tomorrow. Or maybe tonight, in case Fred shows up there in the morning.

By the end of Monday, I might have real news to share. *Oh, dear God, please let this work out for Fred. Please let it be so.*

CHAPTER 18

THE JOURNEY STARTS WITH LUCY

Fred

"Repeat it again. Slowly."

Viola squints at the page, her lips moving in sync with the swaying leaves above us before any sound comes out. She's already grasped basic reading, but these senior-one science books are another story, even for her sharp mind.

"The cell me–mbrane... controls what goes... in and out of the... cell." She winces, then glances up for approval.

"Good." I shift on the woven mat, the straw prickling my stomach and pride swelling warm in my chest. "Now again. But this time, say it like you believe it."

She rolls her eyes, then moves her finger along the line. "You sound like a teacher already."

"That's the goal." I tap the dog-eared biology textbook between us, one of Alex's old school books he sent for Viola. "You keep practicing, and you'll outsmart me soon."

She giggles and rolls to her side enough to glance at me. "Then I'll start teaching you for a change."

Is it no longer an impossible dream—her becoming a career woman?

Her dust-covered feet lift into the air as she lies on her stomach, the fraying hem of her dress brushing the mat. She's smart and hungry to learn. She deserves more than the limits this village offers.

Yes, Father meant it about giving me the land. He confirmed it when I asked again just to be sure I'd heard him right. I'd dared hope he'd show the same excitement when I told him Viola could go back to school.

Instead, he frowned. "There's a chance for her to get married while she still has a suitor. Why don't you focus on your dreams for now?"

"Viola." I tug at her wrist. "Don't let them marry you off young, okay?"

Her smile fades, replaced by a quiet understanding far beyond her fourteen years.

"I mean it."

She should be in school already this first term, but the house she'll stay in won't be available until second term. That's less than two months from now, which fits my schedule. I won't start the institute until the beginning of August... if I get accepted.

"Soon, you'll be wearing a uniform and sitting in a real classroom."

"But how?" she whispers, her voice small. "Father already said education for girls is—"

"You and I are going to change that." It's unfortunate we are raised believing girls were for the sole purpose of training to be a wife someday and boys to herd the farm. However, the boys get the chance to finish school through the five years provided in our small school in the village. "We are taking steps that add up to something bigger."

She taps the textbook, running her finger over a diagram of cell structures. "Lucy helped you. That's why everything changed."

"She helped." I breathe out, squeezing her shoulder. "That's why I'm helping you, and you and I can help our younger siblings catch up when the time's right. But for now, we have to be ready to walk into the doors while they are open." And they are now that Lucy's father arranged my interview with the institute. He even convinced them that I can pay the fees in installments. As soon as I get to the city, I'll look for a job so I can study and work to cover the remainder of the school fees.

"When you're in school in the big city, will you always come and visit me at my new school?"

"Your new school is a city compared to our village." Of course, she'll be on school grounds, which will be a luxury in comparison to farming and housework. "Not only will I visit you, I'll call you often. I'll take you to school on my bike and pick you up at the end of every term." I should buy a phone too, as soon as I make some money.

"You promise?" She holds out her small finger, the way we used to when she was much younger.

I hook my finger with hers. "I promise."

But right now, I have to focus on my journey tomorrow. Where I'll sleep when I get there, what I should expect. Lucy only told me what day to come and what taxi to take from Kampala.

"Don't act like you're lost, or you'll draw attention from pickpockets." She gave me a spiel on how to avoid being robbed. "Keep money close. Otherwise, at times, it escapes out of your pockets without you knowing." The only money I plan to have with me is for transport and maybe some extra if I see something nice to buy for her.

Just before supper, I fold my decent shirts for the journey. Double-checking my small bag, I unzip each pocket to ensure the certified results are there. Now I'm not sure how to carry these with me. What if they rob my bag and the certificates vanish along with it?

I groan. Just how am I going to get through this journey? I should've accepted Lucy's offer to meet me in Kampala so we could board another taxi together to her papa's barracks.

"Fred," Mama calls from outside my open door before she knocks and hovers in the doorway, her hands folded in front of her. "I never said I was sorry."

I know what she means. "You said it to Lucy, and she understood."

"I wasn't kind to her. I see why you like her." She names some of the many qualities I love about Lucy. "She's... sure different from our women, and it's clear she likes you a lot. She didn't have to help me."

"And me when I hadn't—"

She holds up a hand. "It looked like you sided with me that day. You should have sided with her."

That confrontation still stings—Lucy walking away hurt, me caught between loyalties. "I already asked her forgiveness." And Lucy has a generous heart. "Thankfully, she's quick to forgive."

Mama presses her lips together in a mixture of regret and determination, her eyes distant. "I watched your father push you out of your home. I agreed with him about you marrying Safiri. I should have stood up for you."

"No, Mama, you're a traditional woman. No one expects you to speak against your husband."

My throat tightens. The fact that she wants to go against tradition—for me—is enough.

I walk over and wrap my arms around her. Her arms don't return the gesture, but that's okay. We're not a hugging family. Still, I savor the moment—the faint scent of woodsmoke and laundry soap clinging to her clothes, familiar and comforting in a way that chokes me more than I expect.

"What are you doing?" she asks.

"Hugging." I step back.

She blinks, confused.

"It's something people do when words aren't enough."

"I like it." She then steps forward and wraps her arms around me.

This time, I hug her back tight, and our silence is full of all the words we've never said.

"When Lucy comes back to visit her family, bring her."

"I'm not sure Father and her papa are on the same page."

Mama draws back and cups a hand to my face. "Maybe it's time to start making things right."

"I can't agree more."

The Big City

Fred

I'm not sure what I expected, but Kampala doesn't have gold-paved streets. I realize that with every jolt in my seat as the car lurches from one pothole to another. The roads are mostly paved, but some are riddled with holes and dirt patches.

The sidewalks are crowded—vendors everywhere. Food, clothing, and bright necklaces dangle from wooden boards like a street market bursting at the seams.

I lean toward the window like Lucy advised.

The farther we go, the louder it gets. The roads widen, but so do the traffic jams. Cars squeeze past each other, honking, wheezing, coughing up smoke. I've never seen this many motorcycles in my life—some weaving between taxis, others parked in long rows on the sidewalks, waiting.

The conductor cracks a window, and the smell hits me—diesel thick in the air, tangled with sweat, fried food, and something else I can't place. Signs hang off every building like the city is shouting in five different languages.

I paid my fare as soon as I boarded, too nervous to fumble with money later in front of strangers.

I've kept the paper with Lucy's instructions tucked in my shirt pocket. Now, I pull it out and unfold it to her tidy writing:

In the taxi park, look for the sign with cars going to Kabesa. If the taxi drops you off by the clock tower, take a boda boda straight to the police barracks.

I'm so grateful when the taxi drops me off at the park. I keep my head down, avoiding too many questions, not wanting to look lost.

White vans with blue stripes flood the lot, rows upon rows. I scan the signs above them and weave through a sea of moving bodies. Everyone seems to be rushing like they're late for something life-changing.

"You should buy this!" A merchant thrusts a handful of shirts in my face, blocking my view. "Take one."

"No thanks." I sidestep and grip my bag tighter. Lucy warned me about the city's aggressive sellers.

Horns blare. Conductors shout destinations and prices over the chaos.

But where's the sign for my next taxi?

Ah, pure relief. Someone calls out the name of my stop, and I spot the sign beside the van as the man chanting the route waves me over.

"I'm stopping at the barracks," I tell him.

"We'll get you there." He points to the open door.

I climb in.

Once I sit, merchants swarm the open windows—sodas, fried foods, shirts, shiny necklaces, and all sorts of things I've never seen sold in my village. I fight the urge to buy a necklace for Lucy. She'd warned me, though—don't pull out money. Next time, I'll be ready. I'll save and buy her something nice.

By the time the taxi fills up, I can barely breathe.

The man in the middle seat is nearly sitting on me, his elbow digging into my ribs every time he shifts.

The conductor shouts. "Scoot back! We can fit one more!"

There's nowhere left to sit. But at least this is the final ride before I see Lucy. The taxi takes off. Within a few minutes, it slows, and the man calls out. "Barracks stop!"

My heart kicks against my chest. I lean out the window and spot a gated housing estate. This is it.

I step out.

The taxi takes off, and I adjust my bag, squinting in the afternoon sun.

"Fred!"

My heart thrums at her voice. I turn, and there she is, racing toward me from the wide entrance to the community.

Her braids are gone. Her natural hair flows in soft waves over her shoulders.

She looks like she appears in my dreams. Only this time, instead of her usual yellow dress in the dream, she's wearing black with big white flowers.

"Lucy!" In one long stride, I toss my bag. It thuds to the rock-patched dirt. Then I'm within reach of her, lifting her off the ground. She smells sweet and familiar, fragrant in a way only Lucy ever is.

"You made it."

"I did."

"Alone." Pride packs that single word.

The tension from the uncertain journey melts away.

"You were with me the whole time."

"What do you think of the city?"

I set her down from the embrace. But her hand finds mine, our fingers interlacing like it's the most natural thing in the world.

"It's very..." A car speeds past. Two motorcycles whiz by behind it. "Your world is loud."

"Soon it'll be your world too."

I pick up my now-dusty bag. She swings our joined hands as we walk into the estate. I should be concerned. Her father won't like seeing us like this. But if she's holding my hand this boldly, the officer mustn't be nearby.

"Are you ready for your university appearance tomorrow?"

I laugh. "I was too worried I might not make it to you to start worrying about tomorrow yet."

"You'll do fine."

We pass through the entrance where several metal buildings crowd alongside the opening.

"Papa is in his office, but he wants to see you as soon as you arrive."

My hand slips out of hers. "He better not catch us holding hands."

"You're right." She gives a sheepish smile. "After the interview tomorrow, I hope I can show you around the city."

"I'd love that."

"You're going to stay at my friend Molly's house. You'll be bunking with her twin brother, Hugh, and she'll stay with me during your visit."

Right, I remember her casually mentioning her friend's brother. Knowing Lucy's close to Molly's brother doesn't sit well. I don't even know the boy, but something twists in my chest at the idea of some guy being part of her world. "What's Hugh like? I mean, if I'm staying with him?"

"He's a good friend. He's nice." She elbows my arm, perhaps sensing my tension. "Sometimes he can be a show-off. But he knows you and should treat you kindly."

Has Lucy spoken about me to Molly and Hugh? There's some sort of comfort in that. I swallow the jealousy while uniformed officers move in and out of two small metal buildings.

I've never seen Lucy's papa in uniform. For all I know, he could be one of the men storming through those doors.

"That big one in the center is Papa's office."

She must've read my thoughts. My gaze lingers on the open doorway. "It's great that your papa worked out those details."

This could be the only time I have alone with Lucy. I pause. "Lucy?"

She glances at me sideways, then stops walking.

"Thank you. For everything. For believing in me, even when I doubted myself."

"You did the hard part, Fred. You studied. You pushed yourself to follow your dream."

"But you were the light showing me where to go."

"God is the light."

"Yes. And maybe that's why I'm standing here right now—about to meet your papa over something that doesn't involve him scolding me about his daughter."

Her lips curl, and it's adorable.

Will I get a chance to sneak a kiss? Maybe.

"Very poetic." She shoves me onward. "Now come on. Let's go see Papa. I'll show you around the community after."

As we head toward the building, I should be panicking. But it's hard to feel afraid with Lucy striding beside me.

So much is still uncertain, but my chest—my whole world—expands. I'm not just a village farm boy anymore. Not when I have a city girl who's becoming a doctor someday, and neither of us is willing to choose between love and dreams.

We're choosing both.

CHAPTER 19

The Scary Unknown

Fred

My mind whirls as Lucy leads me to Mr. Jenga's house.

After supper with her papa, the three of us sat before Lucy suggested we tour the barracks.

"I need to escort him to his quarters," the officer said.

But Lucy cut in, "I'll be walking back with Molly. Might as well take Fred there after the walk."

Now, Mr. Jenga's house comes into view. With its red roof like the officer's, but smaller. Lucy already explained why her papa's house is the biggest—being the officer grants that privilege. Still, Jenga's place looks solid compared to the metal-framed homes crowding the rest of the compound.

I slow our stride. "I've never seen so many homes packed so tightly together."

"It's not too different from the kind of housing you might stay in during your studies. There's plenty of affordable housing options near the institute."

"Your papa said your friend and her brother are going to the same institute?"

She nods, her gaze drifting toward the horizon where the sun dips behind tall trees above the rooftops. "All the more reason it's good you'll meet them tonight."

We barely step onto the narrow path leading to the house when the door swings open and a girl about Lucy's age rushes toward us.

"Lucy! Fred!"

In white shorts and a pink blouse, her hair short and curled, she throws her arms around Lucy, then leans in to whisper into her ear, sharing some a secret. She then turns to me, her smile kind, before she hugs me. "So nice to finally meet you."

"Very nice to meet you too, Molly. Lucy always talks about you."

My heart warms as I hug her back awkwardly, but not too stiffly. Lucy's taught me how to hug. Seems like it's normal here.

"I'll take your bag." Molly snatches it as soon as the embrace ends. "Lucy and I already picked out a film for you to watch tonight."

I blink. "A movie?"

"The pictures on TV." Lucy slides her hand into the crook of my arm, reminding me of the screen running at her house with people talking. "We picked one of our favorite films for you."

"Oh." I don't know what to expect from a film. All I know is what Lucy told me. Including her best friend, Molly. I don't remember her talking about Molly's brother, though. Maybe that's how irrelevant he is to her?

"Our television isn't as big as Lucy's," Molly chimes in. "We usually watch at her place, but I told Hugh to let you use ours tonight."

"You didn't have to do that." How great to know Lucy has a friend like her.

"I want you to get acquainted with city life," Lucy whispers, her breath warm against my cheek.

"I already have the girl I want from the city. What more could I need?"

"True." She leans into me, and I savor her nearness.

"You two." Molly tsks, shaking her head.

Molly's kind and sweet-looking, but Lucy steals my breath. Not that I need comparisons. Lucy will always be the most beautiful woman in the world to me.

"Well... well." The voice cuts through the fading light. A boy around my age or Lucy's approaches.

He must be Molly's brother. I can't make out his features, but he's tall—maybe as tall as me, if not taller. He walks with easy confidence and a smirk that makes my arm slide around Lucy.

Not claiming her. It just happens.

"Fred, I believe?"

"Don't act like you don't know it's Fred." Molly kicks his shin.

He winces and mutters something about putting a lizard under her pillow.

Lucy laughs under her breath. "I forgot to mention. He can be dramatic."

Still, I don't like the way he looks at Lucy like he's sizing something up.

"So you're Fred." His eyes shift to me, his voice smooth as oil. "Lucy told us all about her farm boy."

No way Lucy called me that. I ease my arm off her and extend my hand. "Nice to meet you."

He shakes it, his smile not quite reaching his eyes. "You're serious about this teaching thing, huh?"

"Very."

"You think farmers need to learn more about agriculture?"

Although I'm sure he's not looking for answers, I still respond. "I'm not going to teach agriculture—"

"Fred, you don't have to answer to Hugh." Lucy steps forward and jabs a finger into his chest. "What's wrong with you? I just told Fred you're nice, and shame on me for thinking that was still true."

"I am nice, Lucy." Mock-wounded, he presses a hand to his heart like he's in a play.

I don't like how comfortable she is with him, how easily she touches him, even if she's angry with him on my account. Hugh doesn't even flinch. They know each other too well.

"Why don't you have the front light on?" The deep voice cuts through the dim air, and we all step apart.

"Father!" Molly calls out.

The man smiles, walks up, and hugs her, his form broad and calm in the fading light.

Hugh moves in to shake his hand.

"Get the visitor inside, will you?" Mr. Jenga extends his hand. "I'm their father."

I straighten up, aware of how much space now separates Lucy and me. Then I introduce myself, though he must already know my name and why I'm here. His eyes are kind, which I see more clearly when we step into the house and the light overhead fills the room.

We settle into the chairs. The pillow beneath me shifts every time I do.

He nods at Hugh. "Fetch our guest a soda."

This guy will for sure be smirking while playing servant, so I hold up a hand. "I already ate at Lucy's house, sir."

Lucy and Molly disappear down the hall, their laughter resounding behind them.

Mr. Jenga then asks what I think of the city, his eyes steady and genuinely curious. I answer, giving just enough without sounding like I'm trying to impress him.

"That's the kind of determination I like to see." He nods to Hugh lounging across from us, legs spread wide. "It's good you'll both be at the same campus. Maybe Fred can rub off on you."

"I already know everything about farming from agriculture class, Father." Hugh gives me a sideways smirk. "I'll be studying business. No need for farming lessons."

"I'm talking about focus. Drive. You need friends who push you."

"I have enough friends, Father." He stands and leaves the room.

My stomach coils. The confidence I walked in with slips.

Lucy and Molly reappear from the hall. Their laughter fades. Perhaps they caught sight of the tension.

"We put your bag in my room," Molly says, then clarifies. "That's where you'll be staying."

As she says good night to her father, Lucy gestures toward the small screen on a tall stand in the corner. "I can turn on the movie for you if you want."

I hadn't taken time to look around the room. A photo of Mr. Jenga in uniform hangs on the wall, and another of him with a woman who looks like Molly and Hugh—same long nose.

"I think I'll just go to bed early."

"You've got an early start." Mr. Jenga stands and gestures toward the hallway. "I'll show you to Molly's room." Then he adds, "The showers are outside if you need to clean up."

"I showered at Lucy's house." I get up. Their shower is in the house.

Lucy stands at a distance, probably holding back, not wanting to show affection in front of her father's friend.

"Good night, Fred." She winks. "I'll see you tomorrow after your interview."

I fold my hands in front of me, grounding myself, fighting the urge to close the gap between us and hold her in my arms. "Good night."

"I'm going to pray for you."

The girls head toward the door, but Lucy pauses, rushing into the kitchen where Hugh disappeared.

She's back in seconds. I hear Hugh calling after her, wishing her good night.

Now I'm not sure. Did she go in to say good night to Hugh? I didn't hear what she said, didn't see their exchange.

But no. Lucy wouldn't have helped me, wouldn't have arranged for me to stay here if she had feelings for Hugh.

Lucy loves me, not Hugh. I tell myself that again. Then she turns back to wave, smiling that familiar, genuine smile, and my doubts dissolve.

I wave back. She steps out of the house, their muffled voices drifting through the closed window.

"I'll walk them over. If you need anything... Hugh!" Mr. Jenga calls toward the kitchen.

Hugh emerges, biting into a piece of bread.

Mr. Jenga nods to his son. "Help Fred if he needs anything."

"Lucy and Molly said you need to watch a romantic film." Hugh walks over to the TV. His voice softens a bit. "I was warned not to change anything."

"I don't need to watch any films, but thank you."

I don't want to trouble anyone, but I was never shown where Molly's room is. I gather the nerve to ask.

"Down the hall to the right."

When he gestures the way, I thank him and wish him good night.

The mattress is three times more comfortable than my usual thin pad. But between the unfamiliar room and Hugh's unpredictable attitude, which, to be fair, improved before I went to bed, sleep doesn't come easy.

Of course, my mind is also spinning with thoughts of the interview. What kind of questions will they ask?

I close my eyes and think of Lucy—our parting words echoing back.

Prayer.

Yes, she said she'd pray for me. So I pray for myself too, whispering into the dark, unsure if I'm doing it right, but meaning every word.

Somehow, sleep finds me. I wake to a knock just as the door opens.

"You're going to be late," Mr. Jenga calls. He's already dressed in uniform, glancing at his watch as I sit up.

"What time is it?" I cover my mouth as I yawn.

"You still have fifteen minutes to eat something before getting dressed."

I glance down at my shorts and T-shirt. I'll be changing into the navy button-down Lucy made for me—one of two she sewed herself. She even bought me a few more shirts over the year since we met, expanding my wardrobe.

I'm meeting the officer at his office, and we'll go from there. Mr. Jenga will be taking me. Otherwise, I'd get lost in this crowded community.

Within minutes, I'm seated at the table with Mr. Jenga and Hugh, eating slices of bread smeared with butter and sipping lukewarm milk.

"Nervous?" Hugh catches me off guard. He actually looks serious, sincere, even.

"A little."

He grins. "If you're as smart as Lucy says, you just need to speak like you mean it."

"Thank you." I swallow, surprised by his sincerity. It's like he's a different person.

Is that what Lucy whispered to him before she left? A reminder to be kind?

I hope not. I wouldn't want her to defend me like that, to make me look weak, like I can't handle myself.

But if she did, she meant it with good intentions.

"Hugh and Molly have their interview at the same university next week." Mr. Jenga pours himself more milk. "That's why I rushed them back from their mother's, to help them prepare."

"I'm sure you'll do fine too." I reach for my tea and take a sip.

Maybe Hugh is a decent guy after all. And if Lucy talks about me to him and Molly, maybe I shouldn't be so tense just because he's spent more time in her world than I have.

CHAPTER 20

THE INTERVIEW

Fred

My palms are damp. I rub them against my pants as silence stretches.

The principal squints at my transcripts, lifting his glasses to get a better look. To his side, a younger man in glasses shuffles papers, scribbling and stamping without glancing up. Beside me, the officer's briefcase brushes my leg where it rests on his lap.

I shift my gaze to the off-white walls lined with framed photos of the campus through the years. One picture shows an old single building, the next, a second wing added. The most recent frame displays rows of solid brick structures. Growth.

"You scored well on the UCE." The principal's voice draws me back. "UACE... excellent. But math knocked you out of the sponsorship bracket."

"He's bright and dedicated," the officer chimes in, his chest lifting.

Is that pride in his voice? Did he forget I'm his enemy's son?

"If he managed results like these after missing years of school," he continues, "imagine what he could do with a full education."

Now, I'm too hot. I shift in my seat, unsure what to do with all the praise.

He keeps going, telling the principal how I'm the kind of student this campus needs.

"I can tell he's someone we want." The principal adjusts his glasses and folds his hands over my results. He cocks his head to one side, and the light catches the gray peppering his tight curls. "Why teaching?"

I straighten, grateful for a question I know how to answer.

"No one in my village studies beyond primary five. I want to change that." I meet his gaze. "If kids like my sister are going to become something, I need to bring learning to them."

The questions then come rapid-fire about discipline, teaching methods, classroom management, and I answer from my gut. From what I've seen at John's school. From everything I wish had been different in my own.

The officer takes over, asking questions I wouldn't have even known to ask, focusing on tuition fees, possible sponsorships, and student-teaching opportunities.

The principal jots notes between glances at my transcripts. Finally, he removes his glasses. "Do you have any questions for us, Mr. Bageya?"

I take a breath. "Just one."

He nods.

"Do I need to stay on campus? The housing fees..." I don't want to sound like I'm already struggling. But I am. Lucy says cheaper housing is available nearby.

"No." The principal folds his arms over his chest. "As long as you live within ten kilometers of campus, you're free to stay off-site."

Hope rises like a sunrise in my chest.

He turns to the younger man, whose name I never caught, and tells him to begin the enrollment process and give me the materials I'll need for August.

Shock doesn't even come close to what I feel when the officer steps up and pays my registration fees, counting crisp paper shillings on the spot. Had he intended to do this all along? Or did he just carry cash around for no reason?

Outside, as we step onto the red-stone path, I manage. "Thank you, sir."

He shrugs. "If you don't register, they could easily give your spot to the next person who commits."

He's tall, and next to his long strides, I feel like a child just learning to walk. "I'll pay you back as soon as—"

"Consider it a gift for finishing advanced level."

I blink, stunned. "Thank you."

"You'd better study hard so you don't waste my money."

"Yes, sir."

Outside the campus gates, I stay close to the officer, who grips his briefcase under his arm, ignoring the swarm of motorcycle riders urging us to hop on.

They're aggressive—shouting out destinations, trying to win us over. City business is... intense.

We push past them and catch one of the many taxis calling for passengers.

It's a fifteen-minute ride back to the barracks. The officer made it clear I'd be leaving as soon as I finished my interview. He didn't state it that way, but he asked if I could take a few things home to his wife today, his way of saying my work in the city was over.

But when we return to his office, he hands me my bag. "If you leave without saying goodbye to Lucy, she'll be asking to return to the village for another holiday."

His voice is softer than I'd ever heard it. Does he know I'm the reason she keeps wanting to go back?

I scratch my head.

He holds up a hand. "I'm going to assume she came to the village to support you... to help you get into school."

"I think so." I nod. What else can I say? Is he testing me?

"Lucy will escort you," he continues. "She knows what I want her to pick up for her mother. Once she's done, she'll take you to a taxi that won't make any stops until you get into the main town."

Town, where Gertrude and John live. From there, I can catch a bus or pay a bicyclist to take me the rest of the way home.

I'm just glad I get to see Lucy again. I get to say goodbye properly.

The officer grabs his briefcase and ushers me to the door.

"Wait."

I pause in the doorway as he opens the briefcase and pulls out my transcripts, now neatly placed in a manila envelope.

"Keep these very, very carefully," he says. "You lose them, and there's nothing to prove you ever went to school."

My hut could catch fire. Anything could happen.

"Would it be okay if... you kept them for me?" The words slip out before I can stop them.

He's had kids in school. He knows how to store these things.

More than that, he just represented me—like a parent—so I could get into school.

He pauses, hands hovering between the envelope and his open briefcase.

"I don't have anywhere safe to put them," I admit.

He nods, understanding in his eyes... maybe even surprise etched across his brow.

I hope I've made the right decision. What if he changes his mind about me—about me and Lucy—and tears my papers out of anger?

No.

He wouldn't.

Would he?

The midmorning sun filters through the trees as we cross the compound.

The officer waves and greets people we pass. The men in uniform bow slightly in respect, while most of the women kneel, though some don't.

His uniform looks like the others, but it's marked with several decorated buttons—some on his chest pocket, others on both shoulders. Clearly, his rank speaks volumes.

Up ahead, Lucy is slapping dust from a rug. When she spots us, she tosses it aside and breaks into a sprint. She hugs her father. "Thanks, Papa, for taking Fred."

Then she turns to me, lips twitching with a stolen glance. "How did it go?"

"I'll let him tell you." Her father strides ahead, giving us space.

Minutes later, Lucy has changed into a full white skirt and a floral blouse with delicate blue flowers. The blouse hugs her waist, soft and elegant.

We walk out of the barracks, and I tell her how kind her father was during the interview. "I doubt my father would've spoken on my behalf like that."

"He admires you."

I snort. "Let's not forget last year he wanted to throttle me."

"You have similar dreams to what he had at your age." Lucy swings the bag she insisted on carrying. "He worked hard to get to school, paid his way, and made something of himself. He sees that in you and knows you'll make it too."

Everything about today feels surreal—even the idea that her father might admire me.

"I hope he respects me enough. I... asked him to keep my transcripts safe."

"You trust him?" Her eyes light up. "You two have an unspoken language. You don't even realize it."

I tell her my concern that he might get angry with me one day. I hadn't thought it through until after I handed him the envelope.

"He wouldn't destroy your transcripts." She squeezes my hand and laughs. "Unless you become a criminal, and he thinks you're not capable of making a difference in the world." Then she gets more serious. "He likes the idea of you someday talking about him in the village, of being the one who gave you hope and helped you bring it back to your community."

Lucy doesn't hug me until we've stepped out of the barracks and are waiting by the roadside for a taxi. Then, with her arms around me, she whispers, "I'm so proud of you."

My bag presses between us, but I hold her tightly anyway.

The officer didn't tell her to show me around the city, but she doesn't seem worried about getting home late. She wants me to see everything—again and for the first time.

We stop at the grounds of a fancy hotel, its entrance framed by towering palm trees and lush green cut grass. We sit in a hut with a thatched roof, shady and breezy.

She orders us chips and fried chicken. I've eaten chicken before but never fried like this—golden, crispy, full of flavor.

We lie back on the soft grass under the shade, listening to birds chirping in the trees and bees buzzing over flowers in the nearby garden. We discuss rental costs and the best locations near campus and when we'll speak next by phone.

Always three steps ahead—my Lucy.

Later, we walk hand in hand through the bustling streets. Vendors call out from stalls stacked with mangoes, pineapples, roasted groundnuts, sandals, and what Lucy calls knockoff watches. The scent of grilled meat mixes with dust and hot oil. People weave around us like flowing river water—everyone in motion, everyone with somewhere to go.

She leads me to a corner restaurant and orders again—chips, more chicken, two cold sodas in glass bottles. "This"—she lifts her soda—"is a celebration."

I smile, still not fully believing it.

"You've been admitted to college, Fred."

I clink my bottle to hers. For the first time, I feel like I belong in her world.

We finally make it to the boutique just as daylight starts to fade. Rows of clothes and shiny necklaces that sparkle like they belong in a different pack of the shop.

Lucy heads straight to the counter and pays for a necklace. She tucks it into a zipped pocket of my bag. "Papa already picked it out. I just had to come pay for it." Then she adds two pairs of earrings—one for her mama and one for Gertrude—and slides them into a different zipper. "I hope your bag doesn't get stolen. Pockets feel safer sometimes, but in a crowd, it's easy for someone to grab something right out of them too."

"How do you survive in a city like this?"

She winks. "By doing your best to stay alert."

Before walking me to the taxi stand, she calls Gertrude and puts the phone on speaker.

"If he hasn't left the city yet," Gertrude says, "he'll have to stay at the shop tonight. Now, hurry before he misses the last taxi."

"We don't want a repeat of the last time we missed a taxi." I frown at Lucy.

She laughs. "Only this time, I don't think your parents are expecting you back tonight. And I doubt you're relying on your papa."

We both laugh. What a mess followed after we missed that taxi. Back then, it ended in a beating for me, and Lucy being told she'd never return to the village. Somehow, everything's changed.

She can come back now. She just doesn't have time.

But I know the way to the city now. I know how to find her.

And I'm moving closer. My life is moving forward because I knocked on the door—well, in this case, Lucy knocked for me. And someone said, "Come in."

CHAPTER 21

CLOSEST ISN'T ALWAYS CLOSER

Lucy

The heat shimmers above the Kampala streets, making buildings waver like mirages. My classes begin in four weeks, and I'm grateful to have some downtime now that my shadowing at the hospital has ended. I could've continued, but I needed to shop and refresh before diving into serious learning. For Fred, Molly, and Hugh, there's just one week left. I secured Fred a place two weeks ago with a 10 percent nonrefundable deposit.

"I still wanted that place." Hugh's voice rises over the vendors shouting prices as we push through the crowded market. "Did you see the restaurant right across the street from it? Leave it to Molly—we'll never find anything at this rate."

"We can barely get through here." I twist sideways to avoid a man wheeling a heavy barrow straight at us. "We're lost if we ended up in the market."

"That's why we brought you, Lucy," Molly calls from behind.

Stuck in the middle of the group, I can hear Hugh's irritation and Molly's sass, though they probably can't hear each other over the noise.

We finally emerge from the crowded market, and a faint breeze cuts through the thick heat. I fan myself with one hand, the other sliding into my skirt pocket, making sure I still have my transport fare. While we squeezed through that crowd, anyone could've slipped a hand in and taken it.

The scent of roasting maize drifts through the air, tangled with exhaust fumes from two taxis idling nearby. Boda bodas roll forward, their drivers eyeing us like we're about to choose one.

We point across the street to the row of buildings. If any of these places are still available this late in the season, either they're overpriced or there's a reason no one's taken them yet.

"I should go with the hostel and forget this." Hugh groans, wiping his forehead with the back of his hand. Sweat darkens his polo shirt collar.

"You're a little late for hostels." I already checked every affordable one near campus for Fred. The decent ones were full two weeks ago.

"Lucy, you'll like this place a lot better." Molly tugs at my hand. Her brown skin glows in the sunlight. "Hugh only wanted that dump because of the food deals posted out front."

I smirk. "Figures."

We wait for more motorcycles to rattle past on the bumpy dirt road before crossing.

"You two are ganging up on me now." He kicks a loose stone ahead of him. His hands are shoved deep in his pockets like he owns the street. "Three buildings I liked, and she's found something wrong with each one—too noisy, too far from campus, too many neighbors with children."

"Children are wonderful." My heart softens as I think of my younger siblings.

"But they're loud. Especially when we're trying to study." Molly loops the hem of her brown dress through her belt to keep it from sweeping the dust.

"At least you two get to choose where you live." I link my arm with hers. "I'm sharing a room with three people."

I toured the place last week and met my roommates. The housing isn't fancy, but Papa paid a fortune to secure it. I hadn't realized how much of a privilege it was until I learned how many people applied and didn't get in.

We arrive in a neighborhood of mixed housing. Some are gated hostels, others simple rentals with no fences.

"This place has running water, Lucy. The bathroom's inside too." Molly quickens her pace toward a narrow path leading to an L-shaped compound.

Flowers blooming along the edge of a cream-colored building add a cheerful touch that makes up for the chipped paint. It's a single-story unit, probably split into four apartments—three doors visible from the front.

"I'll go get the landlady." Molly marches toward a separate house tucked behind the main building.

While she knocks, I wait on the grassy compound with Hugh. "There's a market nearby for your food, Hugh."

He rolls his eyes.

"I actually like it." I shade my eyes, taking in the veranda with its posts separating each entrance. "Fred's house is just a boda boda ride from here. If I visit him, it'll be easy to swing by."

"Did you have to get your boyfriend a place this close to us?" he grumbles, his tone teasing. "As long as you bring him here instead of you two getting cozy somewhere alone."

"You sound like my brother."

"Well, I am your best friend's brother. Someone's gotta keep an eye on you."

"You don't have to worry about me."

He lifts a hand in a mock salute. "True." His lips press into a flat line. "Just come visit us often, yeah?"

"You can count on it."

In all honesty, he's a nice boy. After I reminded him to be nice to Fred, Hugh must've listened because Fred told me how nice Hugh was the morning of his interview. I can imagine being from the village would make it hard for Fred to fit into Hugh's or other people's worlds on first impression.

Ever since Fred's interview at the university, we've only been able to talk over the phone. I'd hoped to use my siblings' first-term holiday as an excuse to visit, but Papa suggested they spend their two weeks off at his workplace instead. Mama came too to spend time with us.

It was good to see everyone—even my half siblings, though they didn't stay the night. During those two weeks, we visited the new church Mama discovered, and I've been going ever since. Once I settle into my dorm, I'll start looking for a church of my own nearby.

The landlady lets us tour the two-bedroom apartment—complete with a bathroom, a kitchenette, a sitting area, and a back door to a narrow veranda.

Her gold tooth flashes in the light when she smiles, hands animated as she points out upcoming upgrades—a security gate, a communal clothesline outside, maybe even flowering plants.

Molly and Hugh list what they'll need. Hugh wants a loud music system and a television since the place has electricity. Molly's dreaming of a long kitchen table, a bookshelf, and a cozy sofa by the window.

As we step out onto the veranda, two girls walk past—one wearing heavy makeup, the other in a skirt so short it barely counts. Hugh's gaze lingers too long.

Some things never change.

"We'll go ahead and pay the deposit," he says, not even glancing at the landlady until the girls disappear into the apartment next door.

"I knew you'd like this place. Why were you giving me such a hard time?" Molly smirks.

I try not to laugh. "You should take it. It's a great deal. Especially compared to what Papa's paying for my dorm."

In the meantime, I'm most excited to see Fred in two days. By God's grace, he sold the land in exchange for a cow and then sold the cow. With the partial sponsorship Papa secured on his behalf through the school, the money from the sale should cover Fred's school fees and rent for the year.

CHAPTER 22

THE CITY DOESN'T CARE

Fred

Anticipation to see Lucy rises in my chest as the taxi slows among the crawl of cars. Panic for the unknown stirs beneath it, twisting through me as I peer through the grimy taxi window.

The capital city looms, alive and crowded. Vendors take up the shop verandas, their goods spilling into the street. Boda bodas weave between honking taxis and cars. People walk in every direction, brushing past one another like a restless tide. The crowd, the noise, it all spins in my head, leaving me lightheaded.

Diesel fumes hang thick in the air, coating my tongue. My shirt is damp, and I attempt once again to shift in my seat for any gasp of air. But I barely move, hemmed in and crushed into the seat, four people where there should only be three.

I clutch my bag tighter on my lap, the only thing I can control. It holds everything tied to my dreams. Finally, all my hard work will begin bearing fruit.

"With this kind of traffic..." The conductor ducks, peering through the window over the packed rows of cars ahead.

"Is it always this bad?" I ask the man shifting on my right.

"From one to eight p.m. is the worst."

When Lucy prepared me to navigate the capital, she told me to treat everyone like a thief because the ones who steal often look like the ones who won't. Still, we've been stuck in this taxi together for over two hours, and he seems kind enough, especially when he talked about visiting his daughter in boarding school.

"We won't make it to the park." The driver tilts his chin toward the jam.

The conductor shifts in his rear seat by the door, perched beside a middle-aged woman. "Not if we want to make it back to Jinja for one more trip before dark."

My heart pounds. If we don't reach the park, how am I supposed to find my way there? Lucy showed me the red-painted canteen above the taxi park—the one where she'd be waiting for me.

The conductor starts collecting fares, his hand stretching out as bills and coins pass from passenger to passenger. I help pass some notes behind me, still trying to stay calm.

Two rows away from the front, I can't ask where the canteen is now. I reach into my pocket for my fare. I kept the transport money separate from school fees, which I tucked in my two-handled brown bag. No one would suspect it holds anything of value.

But to me, it holds everything. Lucy's letters. Our photo album. My tiny CD player. Five nice shirts and two pairs of pants. The diary she gave me, now full of poems I've written for her. A smile creeps across my face just thinking about it.

The rickety door swings open, snapping me out of my daydream. I shift the weight of my bag on my lap.

"Get ready," the conductor calls out. "We're pulling over."

My heart slams in my ribs. I know better than to ask where the park is—one wrong question to the wrong person, and someone might follow me.

As the taxi pulls over, a flood of people moves in the opposite direction. Taxis honk, boda bodas sputter past, and the smell of fried food and exhaust hits me like a wall.

The conductor steps down, guiding people out. One by one, they slide past me.

The woman beside me nudges me. "Can I pass?"

"Oh." I blink.

The man on my right is already gone. The taxi is nearly empty.

As I climb out, I muster the courage and ask the conductor.

He steps back onto the taxi's footplate and points. "Cross the road. You'll see the tall banners in the park. You won't miss it."

"Thank you." I grip my bag handles tighter and follow the flow of people.

Horns blare. Voices shout. Engines roar. Dust clouds rise around sputtering motorcycles from the potholes on the bumpy paved road. It's around two o'clock, but everyone moves like they're already late.

I dodge a boda that doesn't slow down. Ignoring the men calling out if I need a ride, I dart between cars inching through traffic. By the time I cross the road, my heart is hammering.

Then I see the banners and shop signs I remember from the last time. Relief floods my chest.

The university isn't far from here. We came from Jinja Road, and if I were heading there directly, I wouldn't have needed to be dropped in the center of town.

But Lucy is meeting me, then taking me to where I'll live.

I blow out a breath, and the chaos, the sweat, and the fear all feel worth it. I continue along the bumpy side street in front of the shops, weaving past vendors and customers. Then I stumble upon a crowd.

A fight. At least, that's what it looks like. Fists flying. Shouts rising. People chanting and arms swinging, most of them probably unsure of what started it. Still, they're in it—swept up in chaos.

I try to edge past, clutching my bag to my chest, both arms locked around it now. The mass of bodies shoves and slams from every side. I keep moving, pushing through the barrage as much as I can. The bag digs into my ribs, then—

My hands feel lighter. Too light.

Broad daylight turns to darkness.

I spin around.

Nothing but more bodies, more noise. My arms clutch empty air. My breath shortens as I stumble out of the crowd, chest heaving, sweat dripping down my back.

No bag. My hands fly to my head as I scan the street. My eyes sting. People walk, sell, shout, as if my whole world wasn't just stolen and tossed into the thick air.

I spin in a circle. Everyone blends in like it's a normal day, and I can't see anyone holding a brown bag.

No—no!

Someone says something, a deep voice from somewhere behind me. A cobbler with shoes lined neatly on a mat.

"Are you all right?"

I stagger toward the man with salt-and-pepper hair, heart in my throat. "I'm new... I—my bag. It's gone." I point back at the chaos, my voice shaky, parched.

His face softens. Compassion fills his eyes. "Pickpockets love brawls. They start them or wait for one. People get distracted. Easy targets."

Easy target.

My knees weak, I grip the edge of the building to keep myself from collapsing. "I should've taken another path. I should've—" The words knot in my throat.

"Where are you headed?"

That question unravels me.

Lucy.

Everything was in that bag. The letters. The money. The diary. My clothes. I'm so glad I left the transcripts with the officer, but still.

My hope for university? Gone.

I stare past the cobbler. The world buzzes around me like static, but all I feel is stillness. A terrifying, consuming stillness.

I'm not meant for this place. I hate this city. Maybe I was never meant to leave the village. Maybe this is the end.

I thrust my hands into both pockets. Left. Right. Back again. Nothing.

I should've divided the money. Should've hidden some in my sock. Should've done—anything different.

My stomach drops. Sweat beads across my nose and slides down my neck. My hands tremble. My vision tunnels. The city spins around me like a hive, loud and merciless. Police hover near where the fight once raged. The crowd disperses like nothing happened.

But something did. Everything happened.

The money I saved from every market trip. From selling the land. Gone.

My throat tightens like rope, threatening my intake of breath. My fingers curl into fists, then unclench as panic sets in.

My father can never know. But what do I tell him when I come home? That I didn't even make it to school? That I lost everything before I even got there?

And Lucy. All her work. Her prayers. Her faith in me.

What do I tell her?

The officer too. After everything, he finally believed in me.

"Do you need to call someone?" the cobbler's voice breaks through.

I blink at him. My mouth opens, closes. Nothing comes out.

"What happened?" someone asks, and I notice the other vendor. A woman on a mat nearby, folding scarves, leans forward. There's more vendors next to her, and a massive fruit stand along the row.

"He got robbed," the cobbler answers, his voice like a balm over my cracked world. Then to me again. "Do you have someone to call? A friend? Family?"

I nod slowly. Or maybe I just shake.

I pat my pockets, and he seems to understand what I need.

"Use my phone." He presses a battered cell phone into my palm.

The city is still screaming. Honks. Shouts. Engines. But in my ear, it's just the ring.

Once. Twice. Click.

"Hello?" Lucy's voice slices clean through the noise.

"It's gone." My breath shudders out of me.

"Fred?"

"The money. Everything."

"Where are you?" Lucy's voice rises with urgency. "Fred—tell me where you are!"

"It's over." My voice cracks. "I can't—"

The phone slips from my hand.

The cobbler catches it, lifts it to his ear. "Hello? Yes, he's with me. We're near the big yellow sign on Tilma Road. Just walk straight up. He's safe."

Safe.

But I don't feel safe.

I feel like the ground has opened beneath me and swallowed everything I've worked for. Everything I believed I could become.

CHAPTER 23

The Dream Is Threatened

Lucy

The bright "Congratulations" balloon slips from my fingers, drifting upward from the city's chaos. I shove my phone into my skirt pocket. The lunchtime crowd milling around the canteen blurs past as I lengthen my stride, pulse hammering louder than the surrounding noise. I have to get to Fred.

Please, God, let this all be some misunderstanding.

But I know it isn't. The concern in the stranger's voice... Fred... he could barely speak.

Motorcycles whiz past. Horns blare. Wheelbarrows piled with produce jostle for space. I dodge taxis crammed bumper to bumper, the city pressing from all sides.

"Watch where you're crossing!" a driver yells.

Too close. I spin, heart hammering, and step blindly off the sidewalk.

The boda boda slams into me. My body lifts into the air before crashing down, sideways into a wooden stand. Pain explodes across my forehead. Baskets of mangoes, apples, and bananas burst open, scattering like confetti.

Hands catch my arms, steadying me as fruit rolls across the dusty pavement. My vision tilts. I blink hard. A sharp sting burns my forehead.

Someone grabs my elbow. "Ay, are you okay?"

The world feels tilted, unreal, like I'm watching a film from inside it.

The crowd tightens. Faces blur. I lift trembling fingers to my forehead. They come away red.

"Fred." Panic rises in my chest as memory slams back. My legs buckle, but I wave off the strangers crowding around me. "I'm fine." But my knees wobble. "Thank you." I slide away from the man whose hands cushioned my fall. As he steps back, I push upright, swaying.

I scan the congested street. How far do I still have to walk to get to him? "I—I have to find Fred."

"Slow down." A woman blocks my path, her hand steadying my arm, her voice kind. "You might need a doctor."

"Lucy!"

I whip around at the familiar voice—raw and frantic. Fred barrels through the crowd, eyes wild, his chest heaving. He reaches me in three steps and hauls me into his arms, his touch shaking with relief.

"You're bleeding." He says after the embrace, then brushes his thumb above my brow. His gaze drops to his bloodstained fingers.

"I'm fine," I lie. My head pulses with heat. "Are you okay?"

His forehead presses to mine, and for a beat, we just breathe. Together. And I savor the lingering scent of soap from his shirt, mingled with his natural scent. I feel at home already. For now, I try to forget why we're standing in the city.

Fred resumes fussing over me and fits his palm to my forehead. The warmth steadies my spinning thoughts. His eyes are glassy, and my heart aches for him. He tears his shirt hem and dabs the blood. The cotton grazes my skin.

"You ruined your nice shirt." My voice cracks as he continues with gentle, focused care as if we are alone and he hasn't just lost everything.

"I'll manage." His voice is hoarse, and uncertainty shadows his eyes. "I lost everything, Lucy. All my money."

I take the hand he was using to tend to my cut. "We'll figure it out. Together."

"How?" He shakes his head, defeat heavy in his voice. "How do we overcome something like this?"

"Let me make a call. Then we can sit somewhere and sort things out."

Fred nods, and I step aside and press the phone to my ear.

Molly answers, her cheerful voice a stark contrast to the chaos around me. "Lucy! I wish you were here helping me set up my room." She starts updating me about her progress. "Hugh is settled already, but I told him to keep his speakers in his room—"

"Molly." I have to get straight to the pressing matter. "Can Fred stay with you for a few days?"

"Of course." There's a pause before she asks. "Is he okay? Did the landlord give his place away?"

I glance toward Fred, hovering nearby. I can't explain everything now. "I'll tell you when we get there."

"He can use the spare mattress and blanket we bought for when you stayed over."

I thought Hugh was joking when he said they'd have a mattress and blanket so I had no hesitation in visiting them. I release a breath I hadn't realized I was holding, grateful. "Thanks, Molly." I also urge her to talk to Hugh to make sure he's on board.

"Where you're concerned, Hugh is always on board."

I smile as I end the call, my heart soaring at the genuine friendship I've found—not just with Molly, but with her brother too.

Fred shakes his head. "If anything, I need to go back to the village. Is there anywhere I can find work? I can work until I earn enough for transport?"

I squeeze his hand, turning back to the vendors whose stand broke my fall. They smile as they rearrange their scattered display, stacking pineapples and avocados into place. "Can I help you put your stand back together?"

"I'm glad you're fine," the woman says, and the man nods beside her as he dusts off mangoes and sets them in rows.

Fred and I walk toward Jinja Road. With every step ahead, the weight of silent worry blocks us. It's cheaper to get a taxi outside the park.

"Are you hungry?" I ask as we pass a chapati vendor, the warm aroma of fried dough wafting toward us.

Fred shakes his head. His damp hand rests limp in mine, I squeeze tighter, desperate to offer comfort. I'll get some rolex for supper and take them to Molly and Hugh's place.

The towering building above the city reminds me of a relative I haven't spoken to in ages.

"I have an uncle who's a lawyer." I force hope into my voice as we wait for traffic to ease before crossing. I can't press him about how he lost his money. The man on the phone mentioned a crowd, a brawl. Of course, Fred was an easy target. "I'll talk to him, see if he can help."

Mama doesn't really talk to her brother since she married Papa. My uncle didn't approve of Mama abandoning her career and city dreams to marry Papa. I doubt Uncle ever moved past that, which could offend Papa if he knew any of his kids sought out help from Mama's brother. But this could play out in my favor since Uncle doesn't speak to Mama often, never to Papa.

"You don't have to do any of that, Lucy." Fred's shoulders slump, his eyes downcast. "I can't even afford the transport fare right now."

"You have a place to stay for a few days." Until I work out some details. "You're supposed to start school in four days."

He sighs as we seize a gap in traffic and cross the busy street. "The sponsorship only covered part of the fees. I was supposed to pay the rest."

"We'll talk it through tonight."

I lead Fred to a taxi that's calling for Jinja Road, one that will get us closer to our destination. As the taxi stops and goes, picking up and dropping passengers along the busy route, Fred and I sit, lost in thought. What will I say to my uncle? It's a huge sum of money. How do I even start? "By the way, Uncle, my boyfriend Mama and Papa don't approve of needs school fees for university"? As if Uncle doesn't have his own children to pay school fees for.

I rub Fred's thumb. "We could sell the cow in the village." The one I gave him, although it would take too long, causing him to miss the start of school.

"We can't," he whispers, shaking his head. "It has a calf."

"Then sell both."

"No one usually pays much for a calf."

We could give it away for free. At this point, I'm okay with that loss. Fred, however, obviously isn't.

I'd exchanged phone numbers with my new roommate. Did her friend ever find housing, or was she still hoping for a dorm spot? That money could cover Fred's school fees this year. I'd have to figure out where to live near campus. My cousins... Do they still live in that fancy place near Lugogo Road? Hexa works at Spear Motors, and his sister lived with him while attending an institute for beauty school. I'm not sure that's still the case. Perhaps it's time I reconnect with them. If that works out, I'll still have a fifteen-minute taxi commute or five minutes on the boda boda to campus. Or I can spend thirty minutes walking. It's free.

As for my half siblings—no, I dismiss the thought. They'd help, sure, but not without ensuring Mama and Papa knew how generous they'd been.

The taxi jolts to a halt, passengers sliding out. This is our stop too. "We're here."

We step onto the bustling sidewalk, and I hand the conductor the fare. As we cross the street, Fred's hand clasped in mine, my mind is still spinning. I stop by the chapati stand outside the chaotic market and order four rolexes for supper. My appetite hasn't returned since the incidents, but we'll have to eat something so we can all think straight. At least we have Molly and Hugh's place for a few days. Maybe we can talk about hosting Fred for the rest of the year, so we can focus on finding the money for his school fees.

We're still a distance away when the apartment door swings open. Hugh steps out—shirtless, in shorts—glances left and right, then disappears back inside.

Fred slows his steps. "Is this where you're staying? With Hugh too?"

I don't miss the edge in his tone, but we don't have the luxury of options. Why does he feel threatened by Hugh, anyway? "You." I tug him forward. "I'm going back to the barracks." My dorm is ready for me to move in any time, but I haven't felt like it yet. Maybe it's a good thing I haven't gotten attached to my new place yet.

CHAPTER 24

THE ONLY OPTION

Fred

"Would that be all right with you, Fred?" Lucy's hand wraps around mine, her skirt brushing my leg. We're crammed on one chair, but her warmth steadies me. "Just for this year. Until we figure out the next steps."

I nod. The words stick in my throat. I'm still trying to breathe through the hollow left from earlier.

Whoever stole that money better burn with guilt when they touch it. May their fingers blister. May their stomach turn with every bite of food it buys. It's not the right prayer, but right now, I don't care. I want justice.

Not that there'll be any.

This is the city. Nobody's going to track down a thief from a crowd that big. No one even saw it happen.

Back in the village, we never have money for anyone to steal. Maybe a cow, sometimes—if someone was bold enough to drag it off and slaughter it before they got caught. But here? You blink, and your future gets snatched clean out of your arms.

I glance at Lucy. At least, she's still here, her hand clasped in mine. That's something. Maybe even everything.

"Fred!" Hugh's voice cuts through the air. He's finally wearing a shirt—only after Lucy insisted. Molly is crouched on the floor, pulling containers from a box. "I'm going to assume you're okay with the arrangement. The choices are limited."

I nod, though I'm not sure I heard anything past the part about staying here for the school year. All I know is, once I find a job and save enough for transport, I'm going home. There's no reason to stay in the city if I'm not in school. Not even I could convince myself otherwise.

"We'll look at getting you a bed too." Molly stands, a colorful headband knotted over her short bob.

"I'll sleep on the floor." My gaze shifts between Hugh and Molly. "Thank you. For taking me in."

"Lucy's friends are our friends." Hugh's voice is steady this time without the usual smirk.

Lucy considers him a friend, and maybe he considers Lucy a friend too, without expecting anything more. That helps, somehow. But smirk or not, I don't have other options.

"Now that that's sorted"—Molly rubs her hands together—"let's have some food."

Only now do I register the smell, and my stomach growls on cue. The food Lucy bought while I stood there waiting, dying inside, wishing I was the one paying for supper. Will I ever be the one to cover the cost for her?

"It won't taste as good now that it's cold." Lucy hops up to unwrap it.

"Chapati with eggs is always good, cold or hot." Hugh winks at her. "We'd have hosted Fred even without the food bribe."

Odd, he doesn't call me "farmer boy" this time. Maybe he feels bad about the stolen money.

I squeeze Lucy's hand. "Thank you. For supper. For everything."

She doesn't have to respond. Her eyes say it all—she'd do anything for me. But what have I done for her? And when will I ever be able to?

When we finally eat, I place the taste I couldn't name earlier. I've had chapati before but not with eggs, tomatoes, onions, and peppers tucked inside. Even with my low appetite, the flavors all but melt in my mouth.

With the three chairs, they must've planned for Lucy to stop in and visit often. I chew my food and take in the room. Boxes, some unpacked and closed, some opened, still litter the edges of the room, crowding against tan walls that brighten the space. Their father must be doing well to rent them a place this nice. Or maybe all city housing looks like this. I never got a proper look at the place Lucy found for me, only knew it was affordable. I'll have to work extra to pay her back for the deposit she lost on my behalf.

When we finish eating, Molly asks Lucy to help her brainstorm ideas for decorating her room. Hugh stands, brushing his hands off, and offers to give me a tour.

"Let me know if you need to change your shirt." He nods to the rip on my side from earlier when I helped Lucy after she felt faint. I'm not sure if the aspirin Molly gave her eased the pain yet. "Lucy said you'll need to borrow some clothes."

"I'll be okay for tonight. Thanks."

He gestures down the corridor as we pass a half-open door. "Shower, bathroom."

I barely glance inside before following him farther down the narrow corridor.

"Molly's room's that way. And this'll be us."

I hover in the doorway. He points to a mattress still wrapped in plastic on his bedframe—sturdy dark wood. A speaker's on a low table, and a couple of unopened boxes and bags are stacked in the corner.

"I hope the village is loud." Hugh folds his arms. "I like my music up."

The village is the opposite of loud. But I nod. "I like music." Only the songs Lucy and I listen to together. But again, it doesn't matter what I like or not.

When we rejoin Lucy and Molly in the sitting room that doubles as a kitchen, Lucy tips her head toward the door. "I'm going to the barracks, but I'll be back tomorrow night."

Her shoulders sag. Her eyes, usually so bright, blink slower than usual, the skin beneath them faintly shadowed. She's exhausted.

My lips part. I reach for her hand. "I can walk you."

She nods.

We walk side by side toward the busy road where taxis idle and boda bodas hum. Guilt churns in my chest like sour milk. I shouldn't have let this happen. Shouldn't have put her through any of it.

"How's your head?" I glance sideways, eyeing the dark bruise shadowing her temple.

"I've had worse." She smiles in the fading evening light. "Once I sliced my foot while digging at school. Punishment."

I blink. "You never told me that."

"We're still learning about each other."

Her voice calms something in me. For the first time in six hours, I feel the edge of a smile.

"I'm so sorry I lost the money."

"Papa always takes the money straight to school for me." She shrugs. "If I were in your position, I'd have lost it too."

She makes the worst moments feel lighter. Like maybe, they aren't the end.

"Try to get some sleep. You don't have much time left before school starts on Tuesday." Somehow, she's confident, as if she knows something I don't. "You're going to school on Tuesday."

I shake my head, panic tightening every breath. "I'm not going to school." I squeeze her hand and choke out the words with restraint. "I'll try to find work."

We stop at the crossing. Cars and bodas zip by.

"I don't know what kind of job a farmer could do in the city."

She steps in front of me and wraps her arms around my waist. "Let's not worry about work now. Let's talk tomorrow." Her cheek brushes my chest. "I love you."

I hold her close, swallowing the knot in my throat. She deserves more than a boy who lost everything in a crowd. Someone like Hugh, who's sure of himself. Who doesn't fumble in chaos. A boy with money, clean clothes, and options.

She pulls back and studies my face. Her gaze softens, seeing everything, even the words I can't say.

"You don't have to cross." She squeezes my hand one last time. "I'll see you tomorrow?"

I try to speak. Nothing comes. I nod.

She looks both ways, then crosses. A taxi driver raises his hand to signal her. She pauses before she lifts her hand to wave.

I raise mine too. And she climbs in.

The taxi door closes behind her, and I let out a long breath. I can only cling to the hope that tomorrow brings new possibilities. When all is said and done, I just want to be someone worthy of Lucy's love.

CHAPTER 25

CAN YOUR BEST EVER BE ENOUGH?

Lucy

My Sundays aren't usually this busy. As soon as church ends, I make my way to the line of people waiting for the pastor to pray over them.

When it's my turn, he smiles warmly. I bow in greeting. As we shake hands, the metal of his wedding ring brushes against my fingers. He's medium height, probably midthirties, with a calm presence that makes me want to open up.

"I'm glad you still come, even without your mother here," he says.

"I enjoy it."

He asks if I'll be attending the youth conference starting next Wednesday.

"I'll be here."

Fred, Molly, and Hugh will all be in school, and I won't have anything better going on.

"It ends Friday night with an overnight worship and prayer." He winks. "Now that's the real party." Grinning, he lists the food they'll serve on Friday, the band lineup, the worship, and the all-night prayer.

I smile. Sounds like what I need before I start this next chapter. I'll need all the prayers I can get. There's still so much I don't know.

"For sure, I'll come for the food." My heart light, I meet his understanding smile. "I could use some prayers today, though." I tell him Fred's family background and how he lost the money. I don't share my full plan to solve the dilemma. After all, he might talk me out of it. Which won't happen unless God Himself tells the pastor right now to stop me.

He places a hand on my shoulder and prays for God's provision, peace, and wisdom. Peace and calm enfold me as his voice deepens. "You always make a way where there seems to be none. Amen."

"Amen," I echo with renewed hope.

I attended the morning service so I could squeeze all my plans into one day while I was already out. I'd rather not have to lie to Papa about the extra details of my day, and I already told him about church and spending time with Molly.

On my walk home, I detour toward a shady tree. I'm the only one here, save for the open space that will be the church expansion someday.

Pressing the phone to my ear, I wait for it to connect as I bounce my feet, and dry grass crunches beneath my flats.

"Lucy! How are you?" My roommate's cheerful voice sounds on the second ring.

"Hi, Stella." I'm not usually this straight to the point. But time is limited, and I need to cover all my other sources if this doesn't work out. "Your friend, Gigi. She wanted to move into our dorm. Is she still looking?"

"Are you joking? She'd do anything to get on campus. She toured a hostel yesterday but said it smelled like onions and wet socks."

"Well, it's her lucky day." I press a hand to my chest to slow my racing heart. "I'm moving out."

"What? Why?"

"It's complicated." I rub my forehead to ignore the doubt creeping in. "Does she have cash to cover the entire year?"

"Her mama works in parliament. Money's not a problem. She'll even throw in a bonus. They're done stressing over house hunting."

"She can have the spot immediately. Think she can bring the cash tomorrow?"

"I'll call her right now. Lucy, you just made her year."

"Perfect." I exhale. "Tell her to call me back. If possible, I'd like to pick up the money tomorrow morning."

I end the call, lighter already, but there's still one more step. I dial again—this time, my cousin, Hexa.

He answers on the third ring. "Lucy? What a surprise to hear from you! Everything okay?"

"Hey, Hexa. Nothing's wrong." I move around in circles. We don't stay in touch, so of course, he'd know I'm calling in an emergency. I try not to be too direct. "How's Sylvia?"

"Running my house like a general." He laughs about his sister's habits. "You should give her a call sometime. We always have family drama going on." Then his tone lowers. "I'm not sure if Father told Aunt anything yet, but he and I are not on good terms right now."

I doubt Uncle would tell Mama anything about his perfect life spiraling. That's the last thing he'd want Papa to know. "Not really. What happened?"

He sighs. "He wasn't too thrilled when I told him I'm going to court Anne."

"It's nice you and Anne are still together." I can't say I'm not surprised, though. I only met Anne twice. According to Sylvia, he and Anne dated on and off in high school, but Anne is as manipulative as she is beautiful. Sylvia isn't fond of her.

"So, what now?"

"I'm moving forward anyway. I love her. I don't need his money, just his blessing. And if he can't give it, well, that's his burden."

"I can understand." Who am I to judge? I have similar problems. My pulse steadies, grateful for the needed transition. "Hexa, I need a huge favor."

"Anything."

"Sylvia might have mentioned you have extra space." I vaguely explain my sudden need for housing and the complications with the money Papa paid for my dorm. "A friend got money stolen—long story, but I'll explain. Any chance I could stay with you?"

"Lucy, come on. You're family." His voice softens even more when I tell him when I'd need to move in. "Of course. Move in whenever you're ready. Sylvia and I will be happy to host you. She'll be glad to try her fancy hairdos on someone. Anne refuses to be her guinea pig."

"How could I turn down a future hairstylist?" Giddy relief floods me and gushes out in a higher pitch than my usual voice. "Thank you so much, Hexa."

He doesn't even press for details as to why I didn't ask my half siblings for help.

With the way things move the next day, I start to wonder if I should be pursuing business instead of medicine.

I meet Gigi on campus. She hands me the cash—crisp shillings still cool, like they just came straight from the bank.

"I don't even know how to thank you." She passes me an extra stack. "This doesn't feel like enough."

"You don't have to give me more." I dismiss her envelope as I divide the bills into four, folding and stuffing some into the pockets of the shorts under my skirt. The rest, I tuck into my skirt pockets.

"That's a funny way to carry money." Gigi laughs and pushes the envelope back into my hand. Who am I to refuse when I need it?

I hate carrying a handbag in the city. Even though I'm not planning to switch taxis on the way to Kamura University, a boda boda feels like the safest way to get this money to its destination.

The midmorning sun blazes overhead as I walk onto campus. The flowers near the office are in full bloom, in red, yellow, and white further lifting my spirit. Maybe they'd hire Fred as a gardener here if he asked. He has experience, but do they hire students for campus work?

I greet the security guard at the office entrance and explain why I'm here. He points me to the right door. I approach the woman behind the desk—she looks about Mama's age. "I'm here to pay fees for Fred Bageya."

"And you are?"

"Family." I then mention Papa's name since he registered Fred.

Her fingers fly over the keyboard, clicking as she glances at the computer screen. "Are you paying half or full?"

Fred already knew the amount. We got that information when Papa signed the sponsorship letter.

"We're paying for the full year." I rise from my seat and pull bills from my shorts pockets, then my skirt pockets. "Sorry—didn't want it to get stolen."

I slide the folded cash across the counter. "And could I get a receipt, please?"

"Understandable, carrying that much money around." The bills rustle as she counts them, sets them aside, then writes out the receipt.

I breathe in relief when she tears it off and hands it to me. "Anything else?"

"That's all. Thanks."

Exhilaration pumps through me as I leave campus. With the leftover money, I stop by the market across from Hugh and Molly's housing complex—the same market we stumbled into while figuring out a direct path to their house. I buy Fred secondhand shirts, pants, shorts, and even a paraffin lamp as a housewarming gift. It will come in handy during power outages. Much better than the candles they bought. I also pick up meat from the butcher, rice at the stand, and vegetables, something to celebrate properly.

It's almost one o'clock when I reach Hugh and Molly's apartment. I set the bags on the veranda and knock on the open door. The curtain sways in the breeze. I can let myself in, but a knock won't scare them into thinking someone is breaking in. Music blares from inside, loud enough to rattle the windows. Seriously, how is Molly letting Hugh get away with that?

I reach for a bag to step in when the curtain swings open.

"Lucy." Fred's smile is wide, and I'm grateful Hugh loaned him one of his T-shirts. The blue stretches across his chest, and before I can get a thorough look at him, he sweeps me into his arms.

I drop the bag.

"Lucy!" Molly appears behind him just as he sets me down and moves aside. She hugs me while Fred disappears inside with the bags.

"I got you a housewarming present." Following her inside, I fish out the lamp from one of the bags Fred placed on the dining table. "Figured no one planned for power outages."

"This is such a big gift!" Molly shouts over the music, turning the lamp over in her hands like it's the best thing she's ever seen.

Fred lingers nearby, and I point. "That bag has clothes for you."

"Thanks." His lips press into a thin line. He then falls quiet. Is it because I brought something?

I move to his side and slip my hand into his. I tip my head toward the bedroom hallway. "What did Hugh bribe you with to let him blast music like this?"

"We struck some silly deal this week only." Molly rolls her gaze to the ceiling. "I'll tell you later."

"I brought some meat to celebrate." I nod toward the bags. "We'll need to cook it soon."

"What's the celebration?" Molly drops onto a chair, chin in hand, eyes curious.

"Let me talk to Fred first." I walk toward the front. He follows, and we sit on the veranda.

Behind us, Molly yells for Hugh to turn off the music and come help with the cooking. The sudden silence brings a small relief. My heart's already loud enough, thudding over how Fred will perceive all this.

"I have news." I pull out the folded receipt before we sit, our feet resting on the step.

"What kind?"

I hand it over. "Your school fees for the year—they're paid."

He scans the paper, eyes narrowing. "Lucy, where did you get this kind of money?"

"It was a miracle. My roommate's friend needed a dorm room." I tell him everything—how it came together, how I felt God was behind it all. "It just... worked."

"Lucy, no." He crumples the receipt. "This isn't what I wanted."

"You wanted to go to school." Heat rises in my chest. "You wouldn't have taken the money if I gave it to you, so I had to go pay it myself."

"I don't want your sacrifices!" He shoots to his feet, putting distance between us like I've burned him. "You've already done too much. What if your father finds out? I can't live with you risking everything over me."

His voice cracks, and his hands fly up in frustration. "You leap without thinking—always trying to fix everything like it's your job."

The word stings more than I expect.

"Fred, please." My voice shakes. I blink hard, ignoring the neighbors across the way now watching from their veranda.

"You shouldn't have done this." He shakes his head like he's trying to knock the thought out. "I don't need you playing the martyr, not after what your father already—"

"But—"

He storms back inside, leaving me on the veranda, stunned.

My heart splinters. I sink onto the step, tears falling.

"Lucy?" Molly sits beside me, her arm wrapping around my shoulders.

Hugh squats in front of us, brows drawn tight with protectiveness that somehow makes my chest ache even more.

"What happened?" she whispers.

I wipe at my eyes, words sticking in my throat. "I paid Fred's school fees." My voice breaks as I explain how I got the money. "He didn't want my help."

"Ungrateful jerk." Hugh's eyes flash. "I'm kicking him out."

"Please..." My lips tremble. "Don't."

His jaw clenches. "He's not staying here if he's making you cry."

"Hugh, not helping," she says.

"No, Molly. He has no right." Hugh's voice sharpens. "After everything Lucy's done? I'll kick him out right now."

"Stop." I hold up both hands. "He's just overwhelmed. That's all."

Molly squeezes my shoulder. "So... where will you stay now?"

I let out a long sigh. "With my cousins. Hexa said I could move in."

"Hexa? The show-off?" Molly raises an eyebrow.

"Maybe he's changed." I shrug. "Either way, I don't have options."

"You're too good, Lucy." Hugh shakes his head, voice thick and somehow softer. He slides beside me and takes my hand. "Fred doesn't deserve you."

"I wish my heart agreed." I sniff, forcing a breath. "I should go home. I don't want to be at the barracks. But Papa's working, so at least I'll be alone. I need to cry it out."

"Stay, Lucy." His grip on my hand tightens. "Molly and I will keep you company."

"He's right." She bumps her shoulder against mine. "You don't have to be alone tonight."

"I won't be good company." I glance toward the apartment. Fred's still here, and I need to think. If Papa finds out, I don't even know what will happen next.

They relent when I insist. I stand, brushing off my skirt.

Molly hops up as well. "We'll walk you to the taxi."

When we reach the road, they cross with me and wait until I'm seated in the right one. Leaning through the door, Molly pulls me into a hug. Hugh follows with a warm embrace that lingers longer, clearly assuming I'll break. Come to think of it, I don't think Hugh or Molly ever saw me cry before. I don't remember crying over anything else, other than losing my baby sister. Fred will always go in the books for making my head spin and heart beat like it's on fire.

"Text us when you get to the barracks," Molly orders.

"Thank you. Both of you." I wave from the taxi, and the conductor slams the door shut.

The taxi is only half full. I sit alone on a bench meant for three. Today, I need this space to myself. The engine rumbles to life, and we pull away. I lean my head back, drained, trying not to replay the last thirty-six hours.

Someday, Fred will understand I did this out of love, not pity. That is, if he doesn't let the school fees I paid go to waste.

CHAPTER 26

THE NAME IS REGRET

Fred

Where do I even go in this house that isn't mine? The strangers I'm living with are Lucy's best friends—Lucy. I swallow hard, gripping the table like it might keep me from unraveling. My mind won't stop replaying what happened.

Lucy acts fast. I think things through. When it comes to choices, she's a gazelle, and I'm a snail.

I didn't see this coming. I press my fingers to my temple to calm the throb behind my eyes.

The curtain yanks aside. Hugh storms in, eyes furious. Molly's right behind him.

"Calm down!" Molly grabs his arm.

He shrugs her off and stalks toward me. My muscles coil, bracing, but he doesn't hit. He just jabs a finger close enough to graze my shirt—*his* shirt.

"What is wrong with you?" he growls.

"Hugh, please." Molly's voice trembles. She steps between us, hands up, but he sidesteps her so he can glare at me. I only let him because he's mad over what I did to Lucy. I'm mad at me too.

"You don't get it, Fred," Hugh snaps. "You have no idea what Lucy risked for you."

"I know what she risked!" The words rip out louder than I mean. Guilt tightens my throat. "That's why I didn't want her to."

Hugh scoffs. He shifts closer, and I step back. If he swings, I might not let him get away with it.

"She did it for you, you idiot. She knew what it would cost her, and she still did it. You think Lucy just throws that kind of money at people?" His voice cracks. "She believed in you more than you believe in yourself."

"Hugh, stop!" Molly shoots her brother a warning glare.

But I'm okay with Hugh being mad at me. Maybe I need someone to say what I'm too proud to admit.

Molly holds up both hands. "Lucy wouldn't want you to do this."

Of course, she wouldn't. Lucy's the reason Hugh thinks so highly of me in the first place. I see it in the way his chest rises and falls beneath that black T-shirt, his fists flexing at his sides.

Shame claws its way up my throat. I deserve every ounce of his anger.

Molly disappears down the corridor, probably heading to her room, leaving me alone with the mess I've made.

"You don't understand—"

"Oh, I understand perfectly." His voice sharpens. "Lucy sees something in you that no one else does. But if you keep acting like a fool, she's going to wake up and realize you're not worth it."

He doesn't wait for a response. Just turns, yanks the curtain aside, and leaves.

His words land like punches. Not because they're cruel—because they're true.

My breath catches. I glance at the corridor where Molly's vanished, then at the door Hugh just stormed through. I should explain. I owe them that much.

I step outside. Hugh's on the veranda steps, elbows on knees, head lowered.

"You ever feel hopeless?" I ask, my voice strained as I stand behind him.

Hugh turns, frustration flickering in his eyes. "That's how I feel right now." He exhales and shifts his gaze to the flower bed. "Lucy can do that to someone, I guess."

"What do you mean?"

He pinches the bridge of his nose. "No one can convince her she deserves better than you."

It hits hard—again, because it's true.

"The sacrifices she makes for you? It's maddening. Believing you'll ever embrace the city. Thinking you're cut out to become a teacher when you're out here throwing her kindness away like trash."

I grip the back of my neck, shame digging in. I needed the honesty. Still, it stings like a bee. "I shouldn't have reacted like that."

"You have no idea how lucky you are." Hugh's voice softens, less anger, more disappointment. "Maybe she made a mistake, but she knew what she was doing. And unless God steps in, her papa is going to find out." He shakes his head. "Lucy needs your support. Not a meltdown. You think she can undo what's done? That money's gone. Your pride won't bring it back."

He faces me again, his eyes narrow. "Either sit here crying like a baby or be a man. You say you love her? Prove it. Finish school. Get a job. Do something good for her one day. But if you give up now? You're not just wasting her money—you're wasting her time and squashing all hope she has in you. And she won't forgive that."

I shift my weight, uncomfortable with how right he is. For the first time, Hugh doesn't sound like a rival.

"You sound like you're on my side." The words come out unbidden.

He chuckles without humor, his gaze shifting to the garden. "I'm on Lucy's side. Always. I'll fight for and protect her, whether she likes it or not. And if you hurt her again, you'd better pray I don't find out."

Fighting for her. Defending her. Protecting her. All the things I should've been doing. Not causing the tears I saw her cry through that window.

Is Hugh just a friend? Or is there something more?

I've never heard of a boy being just friends with a girl before Lucy. Never saw a woman wear trousers until I met her, either. The city... it plays by different rules.

I study him again, his jaw tight, hands clasped like he's holding back. He was holding her hand earlier. Comforting her like she was his to protect.

The thought unsettles me more than I want to admit.

Before I can stop myself, I ask—

"Do you like Lucy?"

The following silence deafens me. I'm not even sure why I asked, especially if I won't like the answer.

Hugh exhales, long and loud. For a second, I think he won't say anything. Then words emerge in a low rasp. "What's there not to like about Lucy? Everyone does." What I wouldn't give to see his face so I can understand the emotion behind his words. "I'm assuming you like her too. Just be glad she feels the same."

He stands, throws me a glance, and walks back toward the house. "If you don't treat her right, someone else will." The words bounce off his shoulder.

Maybe it's all in my head, but it feels like Hugh left more unsaid. Still, I hear him loud and clear.

I slide to the veranda's far end. The noise from the other renters fades into the background.

If you keep acting like a fool, she's going to wake up and realize you're not worth it.

If you don't treat her right, someone else will.

Hugh's conversation replays in my head. And while I don't have anything to give Lucy, the least I can do is be on her side and not against her. Be grateful she's taking a risk by loving me, a risk by paying for my school fees, even when I have no idea where she'll be staying or how she'll tell her father.

"Fred?" A feminine voice pulls me out of the daze. From over by the door, Molly waves. "Lucy knows your heart, even when you're struggling to see it."

Her kindness is almost harder to bear than Hugh's anger and lecture. I nod, unable to speak, the weight of their words pressing down on me, leaving me with nothing but the bitter taste of my own mistakes.

The Moon in Reach

Fred

My first day at the university is a whirlwind. Things I said, the things I should have said. Hugh barely spoke to me this morning, though we walked into school together to pick up our schedules. He's still mad. Can't blame him. I'm mad at myself too.

All three of us ended up in the same classroom.

The professor's already deep into rules, expectations, and strategies to survive the year. I try to focus, pen scratching across my notebook, but Lucy's face etched with hurt keeps cutting through—her eyes, her warmth, her fighting for my dreams like they were her own.

My chest tightens. Now would be a good time to own a phone so I can call her every hour until she gets tired of ignoring me and answers. Or at least have the money to go to the barracks and find her. If we're still even... us.

I need a job. A phone. Anything to reach her.

This morning, I borrowed Molly's phone. Stomach clenching, I dialed Lucy's number—same as I did last night. Both times, it rang and rang. No answer.

"Give her some time." Molly patted my arm. "She'll come around."

By the time class ends, I'm set on finding work—anything that pays. I weave through the crowded market near our place, scanning each stand and shop for any hint of opportunity.

At a canteen with a faded yellow sign, a plump woman hunches over a charcoal stove, stirring a steaming pot. Sweat glistens on her forehead, and she mutters to herself, clearly overwhelmed. It's well past lunch, but maybe she's gearing up for supper.

I approach as she straightens and sets the ladle on a dented plate.

"Aren't you too early for supper?" She wipes her forehead with her apron.

"I'm looking for a part-time job." I explain my school schedule. "I'll do anything."

She eyes the bag slung over my shoulder—Hugh's bag he loaned me, then jerks her chin toward a stack of dirty dishes behind the counter. "You can wash those. Payment's every evening."

She tells me how little I'll earn, but I do the math. By Friday, I'll have more than enough for transport to and from the barracks. From there, I just have to figure out how to get past the officer to see his daughter.

The next two days blur—classes, then dishwashing. Sometimes, when the early supper crowd floods in, I ladle stew and serve customers.

Each night, like clockwork, I borrow Molly's phone and try calling. But the result is always the same.

Voicemail. That's not even in Lucy's voice.

Tomorrow, I'll go see her.

I lie on the mattress, hands folded behind my head, a light bulb dangling overhead. Doubt creeps in. I won't sleep again. I still don't know how to fix things with Hugh, but I'm starting to think he won't speak to me until I make things right with Lucy.

The only small comfort? I overheard him talking to one of the neighbor girls earlier. He got invited to their place for supper tonight. Maybe he doesn't love Lucy in the way I feared. Maybe his protectiveness was just that—friendship.

A soft tap sounds at the door.

Molly peeks in. "Lucy texted."

I sit up fast, hope rising. "Can I talk to her?"

Molly gives a sympathetic headshake. "She's taking a break from her phone." Or from me if she texted Molly and didn't ask for me.

"She's been attending a youth conference. It ends tomorrow with an overnight prayer."

My heart thuds harder. If I let this break go on too long, it might become permanent. "Which church?"

She leans against the doorframe, tapping her chin. "Hugh and I were planning to go."

She invited them, but not me?

Molly must sense the sting because she adds. "As long as you're more interested in the church service than bothering Lucy, you can come with us."

"I'd rather go separately." Clearly, I need God's help. But more than that, I'll need Lucy's forgiveness without an audience—if I even get close enough to ask.

"Good idea." Molly smiles. "Maybe you'll find your answer there too."

I stay up most of the night, writing, composing a poem. I scratch it out and toss it in the trash bin. I then decide to write a letter, letters I keep scrunching up. No way can I even sum up what Lucy means to me in words. It's the hardest assignment for myself, but if I just say these words to her face without writing, I'll not get anywhere past 10 percent. With each word, I remember more clearly how much Lucy's changed my life.

And how much I stand to lose if I don't make this right.

After my classes on Friday, I rush to the market and scrub dishes at the canteen, finishing in no time.

"Eat something." My boss hands me a plate of matooke and beef in groundnut sauce.

She's right—I should. I dig my fingers into the soft matooke and dip it into the sauce, standing off to the side as vendors brush past me, stacking their stands with merchandise. I barely taste a thing, hurrying through each bite before washing the plate and my hands.

When she hands me my pay, I pocket my money and head home to wash up. The house is quiet—Hugh and Molly must've already left for Lucy's church.

Heart racing,, I change into the yellow button-down and brown pants Lucy bought me. I slide the folded letter into my pocket and head out, my steps a blur between strides and a jog as I hurry to catch a taxi.

The ride drags. My stomach is in knots the whole way, and the taxi stops every few minutes to pick up and drop off passengers. It's the cheaper route than heading to the park for a direct ride—but honestly, I never want to walk through the city again. The moment I step out of the taxi, I flag down a boda boda. The excitement of seeing Lucy drowns out the fear of riding a motorcycle for the first time.

The driver nods when I name the church. At least someone knows where I'm going.

I clutch his waist tightly, my fingers curling into the back of his light jacket. He weaves between cars so close, my feet skim against metal bumpers. I think I close my eyes halfway through, convinced this might be the end of me. But if I'm going to live in the city, I might as well start embracing it.

The sun dips behind the buildings and trees as we pull up to the church. I pay the fare with trembling fingers, my nerves now tangled worse than before.

People are everywhere. Youths around my age crowd the compound, plates in hand, eating and laughing. Smoke rises from food stalls like mist over the crowd. It looks like a feast. Shrubs rim the compound's edges, their blossoms brushing the path. Beyond them lies an open space, and past that, homes.

I head inside. The building is at least four times bigger than the open-air church back home. Cement floors. Open archways where doors should be. Speakers tower at the front alongside the stage, and someone's testing a microphone. Loud feedback pierces the air before fading into soft static.

"Hello." A man slides in beside me. Maybe five years older, he has a calm presence. He holds out a hand. "I'm Pastor Bob, youth pastor here at Faith Church."

"Fred." I shake his hand, offering a nod.

"You should join the others for supper."

"I ate already."

As daylight vanishes, the floodlights outside flicker through the windows. Could Lucy be out there? Hugh? Molly? If she's with them—laughing in that crowd of glowing faces—do I have the courage to join in and ask around like I belong?

The lights inside turn on, brightening the spacious place.

Music starts up, a full band. More people drift inside, chatting, laughing, and sliding into seats around me. My gaze keeps darting to the open entrance. Each time the curtain of bodies shifts, I expect to see Lucy. But I don't. The rows fill up. No sign of Hugh either. Or Molly.

Someone leads in prayer. The worship team launches into a full set—drums, bass, voices rising, loud and joyful like Hugh would enjoy. I try to focus, but I'm craning my neck, searching.

Groaning, I force myself to stay still and listen.

The speaker takes the stage. The message is clear: Seek God first, trust Him, and all else will follow.

Lucy's not here. Not tonight.

Where are Hugh and Molly?

The pastor invites those who are weary, heavy with burdens, to come forward. My legs carry me before my mind decides. I kneel near the front with a cluster of others, head bowed, eyes closed.

God... help me. I've made a mess of everything. Please—show me how to make it right. With Lucy. With everything.

A hand slips into the crook of my arm.

I know that scent.

"Lucy," I whisper before I even open my eyes. When I turn to look at her, my pulse stutters.

Her eyes glisten with unshed tears, her hand warm and steady in mine.

We rise together, walking away from the altar. I lean close to her ear, breath catching. "Can we sit together?"

"There's an empty seat by us." Her lips brush my ear.

Us.

Hugh and Molly are here. Okay. That's... okay.

But still, my stomach churns as I follow her down the row.

And yes, there's an empty seat on Hugh's other side. Lucy nudges him to scoot down. Molly shifts too, which lands me beside Lucy.

We don't say much as the night moves on with worship and prayers. Somewhere between the music and the unknown, I find peace with God. But more than that, I find peace in her presence, drawn in by the soft pull of her perfume, a scent that feels like home.

"I'm sorry," I confess during a quiet moment, just in case I don't get another chance alone with her.

Her fingers tighten around mine. She leans in, her breath brushing my ear and sending a rush of warmth through me. "We'll talk. Okay?"

Talk. That could mean anything—an ending. Closure. My heart pounds so loudly that I barely register the rest of the night. Morning light spills in by the time the final prayer is said.

Talk.

When the crowd begins to disperse, Lucy turns to Hugh and Molly. "Give me a minute with Fred. I'll meet you outside."

Molly nods.

Hugh hesitates, his eyes locked on me like I'm a grenade. "We'll be outside," he mutters, still watching me as if daring me to mess this up again.

Once they're gone, I inhale and blurt out the words before she decides to end what we have. "I was wrong. I'm sorry, Lucy. For how I reacted. For everything."

More words tumble out—questions about her father, where she's staying, if she's okay. I can't stop myself.

"Breathe, Fred." She reaches for my hand, pressing it in both of hers. Calm. Steady. "I've learned a lot this week. There are consequences for our actions."

My stomach clenches. Is this it? Is she about to tell me those consequences include cutting me off?

"I've prayed," she continues, "and I've asked God for forgiveness. Whether Papa finds out or not, I'm trusting God will show me His mercy."

I blink, gape. She's talking about *her* consequences, not mine?

"I'm not going to apologize for helping you," she says. "I have no regrets."

"I'm so grateful, Lucy." My throat tightens. "You've done more than anyone ever has for me. And all I did was make you cry… Not exactly the thanks you deserved."

"There's no joy without tears." Her smile is soft, light dancing on her skin like she's glowing from the inside out. "You have a whole village counting on you. Viola's watching you. She needs to see you make it. And our village? They need hope. They need you."

My knees give out, and I sink to the ground.

"Fred?" she asks, startled. "Are you okay?"

I nod, barely. I have to find my voice for this next step, my heart in my throat. I dig into my pocket with trembling fingers and pull out the folded paper.

"I wrote you something." I clear my throat. "Words I couldn't say out loud."

Even the letter feels small now, but I offer it anyway—kneeling on the cement floor, the cold seeping through my pants as I clear my throat to read it aloud.

"'Dear Lucy, the words on this paper aren't enough to explain how much I love you. How deeply I appreciate you. How little I deserve you.

"'Since you came into my life, everything before feels like darkness. You gave me hope—hope that I could dream, that I could reach something. School felt as far as the stars, but now I believe I could reach the moon if I put my mind to it.'"

My voice trembles, but I push through the lump in my throat and keep reading. "'Meeting you is the best thing that's ever happened to me. You make the world better. Loving you feels like coming home to a place I never knew I belonged—until you.'"

She sniffles in front of me.

I keep my focus on the letter. If I look at her, I'll fall apart and never finish. "'You've done everything for me. And while I have nothing to give in return, you remind me that all you want is my heart, my love. My pride gets in the way sometimes. It blinds me to what we have. But I see it now.'" I lower the letter and meet her gaze, saying that last bit that's not written on anything other than my heart. "And I don't want to lose you, Lucy.'"

"You never lost me." Her hand slides over mine. Then she kneels beside me. She takes the letter and places it on the bench. "I figured you just needed time to see your worth, Fred."

A tear slips down her cheek, and I brush it away. Her skin is smooth beneath my thumb, softer than anything I've ever known.

"My worth is clearer when I see myself through your eyes." I cup her face so she can see me—see the truth in what I say. "Please don't give up on me. I won't be perfect, and I'll probably keep fighting you when you try to help me. But I love you. Let me earn your trust again."

She smiles, then throws her arms around me.

I stumble back, catching myself against the bench, and hold her close. Joy blooms in my chest like it might burst.

"You never lost my trust." Her heart thuds fast against mine like the beat of drums in worship earlier. "I know who you are. Your heart."

"I know yours too."

"I love you," she breathes.

And I hold her tighter, whispering the words back. All is well in my world again.

When we finally stand, Lucy folds the letter and tucks it into her pocket. We step outside hand in hand.

Molly lights up, holding a bouquet of orange and white flowers wrapped in glossy paper.

Hugh stands nearby, hands in his pockets, legs planted apart like he owns the ground. No wonder he called me a baby for complaining about Lucy's sacrifice.

"You remembered the flowers." Lucy slips her hand from mine and reaches for the bouquet, leaving my hand empty and cold. "Did you bring the water bottle too?"

"I thought it was just the flowers." Molly exchanges a glance with Lucy.

Lucy turns to Hugh, lifting the bouquet. "You really didn't have to."

"You were upset the last time I saw you," he mutters and shakes her shoulder as if this is something he does on any given day.

My stomach tightens. That was supposed to be me giving her the flowers. I'm the one who made her mad. Or sad. Or whatever.

Lucy thanks him and heads toward the shrubbery with Molly, chatting as they walk.

Now it's just me and Hugh. Birds chirp from a tree nearby to fill our silence. A few take flight. I'd love to join them. Instead, I might as well be standing on hot coals.

He got her flowers?

Even if I had been the one giving her flowers, mine would've been picked from a field. If I could even find one here. Do dahlias grow in the city?

When Lucy comes back, she's still cradling the bouquet like treasure. I can't tell if her smile is for me or the flowers.

This whole friendship-between-a-boy-and-girl thing is still foreign to me. I kick at a pebble, sending a puff of dust up as the question gnaws at me. "You get Lucy flowers often?"

"Not often, but it wouldn't be the first time." He squares his shoulders, and his serious expression gives me pause. "If you're not going to treat her right, maybe it's time she saw what being treated right looks like."

The words hit like a slap. He walks past me toward the girls.

I follow, a warning ringing in my ears.

Lucy and I might be back together, but the mountains between us haven't disappeared. They've just shifted shape.

Book 3 will be coming soon.

If you would like to get notified when book 3 is live, join my Insider team, follow me on Instagram or facebook group below.

-THE END-

Join my Insider Group and get an exclusive Novella, <u>THE THERAPIST'S NEIGHBOR</u>

Join my <u>Facebook group</u> and connect with her and other readers.

In the newsletter and facebook, I share details about future releases, work in progress, sneak peak chapters before I mention them anywhere else.

Listen to my books for free on <u>YOUTUBE</u>

Stay connected with Rose Fresquez

<u>Bookbub</u>

<u>Goodreads</u>

@rosefresquezauthor (Instagram)

website: rosefresquezbooks.com or rosefresquez.com

MORE BOOKS BY ROSE FRESQUEZ

Checkout the Rest of THE BUCHANAN SERIES

1. *First Site*

2. *Something right*

3. *Bright Side*

4. *Short Sighted*

5. *New Light (A Christmas Novella)*

ROMANCE IN THE ROCKIES SERIES

1. *Complex*

2. *Choices*

3. *Beyond Repair*

4. *Stand Out*

5. *Crystal Clear*

THE CAREGIVER SERIES
1. *The Doctor's Nanny*

2. *The Entrepreneur's Nurse*

3. *The Physician's Helper*

4. *The CEO's Companion*

5. *The Investor's Wife*

6. *The Soldier's Trainer*

7. *The Realtor's Attendant*

THE BILLIONAIRE REUNION SERIES
1. *A legitimate Date*

2. *A Sudden Romance*

3. *A Necessary Compromise*

4. *A Genuine Disguise*

5. *A Convenient Marriage*

THE OFFICE HEARTTHROBS

1. *Yours Temporarily*

2. *Yours Blindly*

3. *Yours Forever*

4. *Yours Faithfully*

SINGLE DADS OF MEADOWBROOK

1. *Where I Belong*

2. *Stay With Me*

A NOTE FROM THE AUTHOR

Thank you so much for reading! It means the world to me that you chose my book out of the many other stories you could've been reading.

It was so hard for me to put Fred through losing all his money—but that part of the story is based on something true. It actually happened to me.

Want to know if my father ever found out? Message me on Instagram, email, or Facebook. I'd love to share the rest of the story with you.

I get asked often about my nationality and culture, and I usually respond via email with answers.

For those of you who are not subscribed to my newsletter, I probably haven't mentioned my nationality. I was born and raised in Uganda, and I'm now an American citizen. My dream is to explore all the beautiful states in America and different countries around the world. For now, I get to travel some countries through fiction.

I wrote this story as a special project to remember my parents, who are now in heaven. I wanted to look back at my childhood spent in a small village in Uganda, where I went during my holidays (In america it would be summer break for students.)

This story is part of a young adult series told in three parts. At its heart, it's a forbidden romance between a city girl and a village boy—but it's more than just a love story.

While I'm not the young girl in this book, I wrote her journey to highlight the hidden beauty of the village life, along with its quiet struggles. Through romance, I wanted to capture the joy, the hardship, and the courage it takes to dream beyond what surrounds you.

I wrote this story to honor my parents and the beautiful place where I grew up. It's been fun to write as it brings back those childhood memories.

My dad wasn't a farmer so he traveled for work and would be gone for several weeks. Mama gave up her city life to move to the village after my father bought a house there. He wanted us to have a peaceful place to go to during school breaks. They bought a lot of land, so we had plenty of space to play and make memories. In this story, Lucy has big dreams for her career, while Fred is preparing to be a husband to some local girl in the village.

In the village where I grew up, there's only one school and it goes up to Primary five. (Fifth grade here) As long as you finish primary five, for boys it's time to gain more experience on the farm and start looking for a wife. For girls, it's time to start training to be a wife, fetch water, collect firewood and harvest food, plus knowing all the farm chores, then get married.

My dad was different because he believed in the importance of education. He worked hard so that we could go to the best schools. Not everyone in the village liked this which created a lot of friction between our family and the locals.

It was hard to make friends with the local girls because most were married as early as 14, and they spent most of their time working on farms, which was different from what we did. This book might feel like it's history because of the simple way of living, but life in that small village hasn't changed much. If you've never been to Uganda or third world countries, this story will give you an idea of what life is like in a remote village.

If you enjoyed this story, I have two more books to finalize this young couple as they go through trials that will test their relationship both spiritually and physically.

Thanks again for reading!

Rose

www.ingramcontent.com/pod-product-compliance
Lightning Source LLC
Chambersburg PA
CBHW020052180626
46812CB00006B/2300